Books by Willo Davis Roberts

THE VIEW FROM THE CHERRY TREE

DON'T HURT LAURIE

THE MINDEN CURSE

MORE MINDEN CURSES

THE GIRL WITH THE SILVER EYES

THE PET-SITTING PERIL

BABY-SITTING IS A DANGEROUS JOB

NO MONSTERS IN THE CLOSET

EDDIE AND THE FAIRY GODPUPPY

THE MAGIC BOOK

SUGAR ISN'T EVERYTHING

SUGAR ISN'T EVERYTHING

SUGAR ISN'T

*A Support Book, in Fiction Form,
for the Young Diabetic*

EVERYTHING

by Willo Davis Roberts

J

Atheneum   *1987*   *New York*

Atheneum
Macmillan Publishing Company
866 Third Avenue, New York, NY 10022

Type set by Arcata Graphics/Kingsport, Kingsport, Tennessee
Printed and bound by Fairfield Graphics, Fairfield, Pennsylvania
Designed by Jean Krulis
First Edition

10 9 8 7 6 5 4 3 2 1

Library of Congress Cataloging in Publication Data

Roberts, Willo Davis.   Sugar isn't everything.

   SUMMARY: A detailed description of juvenile-onset diabetes (Type I) using
a fictional form in which eleven-year-old Amy discovers that she has the disease,
learns to treat it and to deal with her anger, and finally accepts that she
CAN live with it.
   [1. Diabetes—Fiction] I. Title.
PZ7.R54465Su   1987   [Fic]   86–17275
ISBN 0–689–31316–0

Grateful acknowledgment is made to the following people for their technical and personal advice, which made this book possible:

From Providence Hospital, Everett, Washington:
Marian Papenhausen, R.N., Diabetes Educator
Susan Naas, R.N., M.S.N., Pediatric Clinical Specialist
Nancy Churchill, R.D.
Karen Wallace, R.D.

And:
Penny Doyle, Director, Chapter 4, Washington Affiliate, American Diabetes Association

And special thanks to the diabetic children (and their parents) who shared with me their feelings, their attitudes, their fears, and their triumphs:
Tom Doyle
Kristin Flatness
Keith Mandel
Carrie Deisher
Samantha Rule

Permission to reproduce the glossary, and the material quoted in Chapter Fifteen from *ANGER: A Message to the Adolescent with Diabetes* by Joan Hoover, is granted by the American Diabetes Association, Inc. Further information available at National Service Center, 1660 Duke Street, P.O. Box 25757, Alexandria, VA 22313, phone (800) ADA-DISC (232-3472).

SUGAR ISN'T EVERYTHING

1.

Amy was so engrossed in her book that she didn't hear Jan's approach until her sister called from just outside the bedroom door.

"Amy! Where are you?"

With a convulsive movement, Amy shoved the plate of chocolate chip cookies under the edge of her bed and reared up into a sitting position, heart thudding. The door opened, and Jan stuck her curly blonde head inside.

"What're you doing in here all the time with the door shut?" Jan wanted to know, looking around the room and sniffing. "I smell chocolate."

"I had a couple of cookies after supper," Amy said. She didn't mean to sound annoyed, but the words came out that way. That happened a lot lately; everybody seemed to irritate her, and especially her ten-year-old sister. "I'm reading. Is there anything wrong with that? And you're supposed to knock before you come into my room."

Jan's blue eyes fastened on Amy's brown ones. "I called. What's the big deal, if you're only reading?"

"I like my privacy, is all." Amy shifted her feet to a position on the floor where she hoped they'd conceal the plate of cookies. "What do you want?"

"Gram's coming," Jan announced. "Aunt Harriet is bringing her day after tomorrow."

Amy scowled, though she liked her grandmother and looked forward to her visits. "How can she? She's in the hospital with a broken hip."

"She's getting out, and Aunt Harriet says she can't go back to her own house right away." Uninvited, Jan sank onto the edge of the bed, swinging one blue-jeaned leg. As usual, the strings of her red tennis shoes dangled, untied. "And Aunt Harriet has to work and can't be home with her during the day, so she's coming here."

"Mom works in the daytime, too," Amy objected. She wished Jan would get out before she realized that the chocolate aroma wasn't from cookies eaten an hour ago, after supper.

"Yeah, but us kids are here to look after her. She

can use a walker, Mom said. And Gram's going to have your bedroom."

The words were said so innocently that for a moment Amy didn't believe what she'd heard. Then her voice croaked. "What are you talking about?"

"Yours is the only one on the ground floor, and Gram can't climb stairs." Jan dug into a pocket and brought forth a handful of Gummy Worms, popping an orange and green one into her mouth. "So you'll have to share my room while she's here."

Dismay and rage nearly exploded inside her as Amy sprang up from her bed. "No! I won't give up my room to live in that pigsty of yours!"

And she wouldn't have a bit of privacy, she thought wildly. Jan talked all the time. She lived in the middle of a mess that could well have been caused by a tornado, and she couldn't keep a secret for two minutes. Like the cookies. If she knew about the cookies . . .

It wasn't that food was forbidden in the bedrooms in the Long household; it was only that Amy had been so hungry lately that she'd eaten more than her share, and she was getting self-conscious about what she ate because people had begun to notice it. Only tonight Dad had laughed when she went back to the kitchen for a snack no more than half an hour after they'd finished clearing away, commenting that she must have hollow legs to hold so

5

much. It was easier to sneak something into her bedroom between meals than to put up with the jokes about how often she ate.

She had a distant understanding of how Gram couldn't climb stairs with a broken hip, but why did it have to be *she* who got shoved out of her room?

"Amy, what are you yelling about?"

Mrs. Long appeared in the doorway, and though Amy immediately felt ashamed, she was still angry, too.

"I wasn't yelling," Amy said, in a tone that almost made a liar out of her. "Jan said—"

"Honey, I know you hate to give up your room, but it's only for a month or two, until Gram can be home alone." Her mother looked the way Amy would look when she was grown-up; everybody said so. Brown eyes, and straight brown hair cut short and easy to care for, clear skin except for a couple of freckles across the nose. Straight, pretty white teeth. The teeth were sometimes remarked upon in a complimentary way, but they didn't make up for not having blonde curls like Jan.

"But I can't move in with *her*. . . ." Amy felt as if she were choking, and her eyes burned.

"Darling, it's the best we could think of. Jan's going to clean up her room and try to keep it that way; I'm sure if you both work at it, you'll get along fine."

"It's not fair," Amy said, close to snarling. "Matt gets to stay in a room by himself."

"Matt's a fifteen-year-old boy, so I can't very well ask him to share with you. And Jan's giving up her privacy, too. It's only temporary, Amy. Be a good sport about it, will you?"

She didn't feel like a good sport. She felt resentment and concern. A couple of months can sound like years when you're only eleven years old.

When her mother and her sister had gone, Amy allowed herself a few stinging tears. After she'd closed the door, and propped a chair under the knob to make sure her bedroom wasn't invaded again, she brought out the plate of cookies and reopened her book. After a while, the crunchy sweetness of the cookies and the exciting adventure she was reading calmed her down, though she was left with a headache.

"Amy?"

She jerked upright again, but the cookies were all gone, even the crumbs. Amy slid off the bed and moved the chair so her brother could come in.

"I'm going for a run. Why don't you come along?"

Matt was the ideal older brother. He was good-looking enough so that she was the envy of her friends. He was smart enough to help her with homework. When he teased her, it was never in a malicious way, and he respected her right to privacy. He never barged in the way Jan did.

7

He was, however, into running, and he tried to get everyone to join him. Amy sometimes had, until the past month or so. Now she felt too tired most of the time.

"I don't think so. I've got a headache," she told him, which was the truth.

"No wonder. You've been cooped up in here reading for too long, and it's stuffy. The fresh air would do you good. Come on, it'll make you feel better."

"Nothing'll make me feel better," Amy said, sounding as sour as she felt.

Matt had brown hair and brown eyes, too, and on him they were positively handsome. He didn't even have any freckles. He studied her face. "Probably not," he agreed at last, "if you're determined it won't. Feeling sorry for yourself, are you?"

Her temper flared. "Wouldn't you, if it was you who had to move in with Jan?"

Matt laughed. "Yeah. But what else can anybody do? Put Gram on the couch in the living room?"

Guilt nibbled at her. "No. I guess I've got to move out of here. But I don't have to like it."

"No, you don't." Matt had sobered, looking thoughtful. "You can make yourself and everybody else miserable. You can whine and complain so Gram thinks you don't care that she's fractured a hip and can't do things for herself for a while. You can make Mom and Dad embarrassed and ashamed of you.

8

But if that's what you really want—"

Put that way, it made Amy ashamed of what she'd said, though she still struggled with depression. "I'm too tired even to carry my stuff upstairs, and Gram's coming tomorrow."

"I'll help you," Matt offered. "Now come on, run with me, and afterward I'll buy you a chocolate milkshake."

Amy allowed herself to be talked into going. She made no response when her father looked up from the paper and said, "Going running with Matt? Good for you." She resented him, too, though logic told her it wasn't his fault his mother had fallen and hurt herself.

The summer air was cool after the heat of the day. She ran with her brother for half a block, then staggered to a stop. "I can't, Matt. I'm out of breath already."

"You can't be. Not in this short distance." Matt could run a couple of miles and it wouldn't even quicken his breathing. "Come on, Amy-Janey, you're good for four blocks, to the Dairy Queen at least."

Amy-Janey was his pet name for her, one he'd bestowed when she was a baby and he was a four-year-old bending over her bassinet. Though he was always nice to Jan, Amy knew instinctively that Matt liked her the best; he was the one who could get her to do things she didn't want to do, like take nasty-tasting medicine or eat spinach. Or run. Except that this time she really didn't feel that she could run any farther.

"I have to go to the bathroom," she said.

Matt sighed. "Okay. Let's walk the rest of the way to Dairy Queen and you can use their rest room."

"Go ahead and run," Amy said. "I didn't earn the milkshake anyway. I'll walk home by myself."

He punched her lightly on the shoulder. "I'll walk with you, have the milkshake, and then run. Maybe tomorrow you'll feel more like running." He grinned. "Anything to get away from Jan, right?"

"Probably," Amy agreed.

She enjoyed the milkshake. Matt was neat about sharing that kind of thing, especially since he did odd jobs to earn most of his spending money instead of just collecting an allowance the way she and Jan did.

When she got home, the rest of the family was watching television and paid no attention when Amy went into the kitchen. She was thirsty again already, so she poured a tall glass of milk, then hesitated over the box of Hershey bars her mother had bought for Dad's lunches. One, or two? She decided on two, hiding them in her pocket so she'd have something to eat later when she got hungry again, without having to make another trip to the kitchen.

She finished her book before she went to sleep,

and then she had to get up during the night—four times!—to go to the bathroom. It was no wonder, she thought crossly the next morning, that she still felt too tired to get started moving her stuff upstairs to the room she'd have to share with her sister.

2.

$\mathbf{T}$he day started off badly because Amy had to wait to get into the bathroom: her mother was in the one downstairs and her father, who was running late for work as manager of the Easy Supermarket, was using the upstairs one.

"Daddy!" Amy pleaded desperately. "Please!"

He came out a moment later, a scrap of toilet tissue clinging to the spot on his chin where he'd cut himself shaving. "Sorry, honey," he said, tousling her hair. "See you tonight."

She was in too much of a hurry to reply. For someone who'd been up so often during the night, the need was certainly urgent, she thought.

Passing the door of Jan's room, she saw her sister

12

standing in the middle of discarded jeans and shirts and socks, along with assorted books and stuffed toys and a half-played Monopoly game set up on the floor.

Amy paused. "You're supposed to clean it up first thing, so I'll have somewhere to put my stuff."

"I know. I'm going to," Jan said. She pulled off her pajama top and dropped it on the floor.

Rolling her eyes, Amy went on down the stairs. She was ravenous, and she could smell bacon from the kitchen. Her mother was sitting with a cup of coffee; she looked up to smile at Amy.

"Morning, honey. Scrambled eggs in the covered bowl, limit of three strips of bacon apiece, that's all there is. Aunt Harriet is supposed to be here with Gram about mid-afternoon, so I'll be home by two. If by any chance they get here ahead of me, make them welcome, won't you? Be sure to get all your things out of the way before then."

Matt was wolfing eggs and toast, working on his second glass of orange juice. "I'll help carry stuff up if you'll put it in bags or something. I'm going to run first. Unless you want to run with me?"

He never gave up. Amy slid into her chair and filled her plate. "No thanks," she said. "Mom, is there any more grape juice? I'm awfully thirsty for grape juice."

"You'll have to mix it. I'll try to remember to pick up some more on my way home." She wiped

13

at her mouth with a paper napkin and stood up. "See you later, kids."

Mrs. Long wrote feature articles for the *Marysville Record*; it was a job Amy thought she'd like to have when she grew up, or anything else that involved writing. She loved to read, but sometimes she felt she would rather write her own books, especially about wild adventures in outer space or distant jungles.

She drank what was left of the orange juice, then mixed up a big pitcher of grape juice. She was so thirsty she drank two glasses before she put what was left in the refrigerator. Fortunately the family was eating in shifts this morning, and nobody noticed how much of it she was using.

The telephone rang when she was filling the fifth box to haul upstairs. It was her closest friend, Pudge Rapinchuck.

"Hi," Pudge said. "Want to go to the park? The eighth grade boys are having a baseball tournament." She giggled. "Danny Crowell's pitching for the Blues."

Amy surveyed the stacks of underwear on her bed, and the load of books that had to be moved yet. "I can't right away. My grandmother's coming and moving into my room, and I have to get my stuff up to Jan's room."

It made her mad just to think about it, and helped

a little when Pudge made appropriate sympathetic noises. "Gosh! Is your grandma coming to stay?"

"Just until she gets over her fractured hip. Listen, why don't you come over, and we'll go as soon as I'm finished?"

"Um—well," Pudge hedged, "Natalie's here. She wants to go to the park right away."

"Natalie?" Amy heard her voice squeak. "How come Natalie's included?"

She didn't dislike Natalie, exactly. She rather envied her looks: Natalie was elegantly tall (while Amy often felt like a shrimp) and had glossy black hair that curled softly around her shoulders. Natalie had only moved to Marysville a month before school was out for the summer. Amy didn't know her very well.

She'd known Pudge (whose real name was Sylvia) since second grade. Pudge was the only person she'd ever fully confided in, and how could she say what she was thinking—about Danny Crowell or anyone else—with a third person present?

"She asked me to go watch the game," Pudge was saying. "I told her okay, and said I'd have to ask you, too."

"How come she asked you? When did you two get so chummy?" Amy dropped a stack of shorts and tops into a box, decided it was full, and reached for the next box for the books.

15

"We went to the movies together Saturday," Pudge told her. "You didn't want to go because you were too tired to walk all the way downtown, and Natalie came by, so we went together. She's nice, Amy. You'll like her when you get to know her better."

"Well, I have to finish this before I can go any- where. Go on ahead. I'll meet you in the park," Amy decided.

She hung up, feeling sort of disgruntled. Somehow she hadn't expected that anyone else would come into their friendship, that Pudge might like another girl as much as she liked Amy. It gave her a fluttering sensation in her stomach.

Before she went upstairs with the first load of her clothes on hangers, she went to the bathroom again, and then was thirsty, so she got some more grape juice with lots of ice in it. That made her hungry; she took time to fix a baloney sandwich. She was carrying it toward her room when Matt came in, glowing mildly. Glowing was what he called it when he ran hard enough to sweat.

He stared at the sandwich, grinning. "Wow! Dad's wrong about you having two hollow legs. You've got a whole hollow body."

"I can't help it if I'm growing so fast I need extra food to keep me going," Amy said, wishing it were true. She didn't seem to be growing much at all. In fourth grade she and Pudge had been about the

16

same height, but now her friend was a head taller. In fact, Amy had grown so little that she didn't even need a new coat for school this fall; she could still fit into the old one. And just this last week or so she'd noticed that her jeans were so loose she almost needed a belt to hold them up.

"Got everything ready for me to carry?" Matt surveyed the accumulation and picked up the biggest box. "Okay, princess, let's move you to the enchanted castle."

Amy glumly followed him up the stairs. Some enchanted castle, she thought. Even when Jan had "cleaned up" you could tell a slob lived here. At least there were twin beds, so she'd have her own and wouldn't have to share that.

She stowed her things in the closet, put the folded garments into the drawers Jan had emptied, and sat down on the edge of the bed to eat. She supposed she'd have to make the best of it.

It should have been fun at the park. Amy would have liked watching the boys play baseball, even if Danny Crowell hadn't been pitching. He was really good, and he could hit, too; besides that, he was cute. He had dark auburn hair that waved, though he often wet it down in an attempt to straighten it out, and on him freckles looked great. He had muscles that bulged when he hurled the ball or swung the bat.

17

Only Pudge knew how much Amy liked Danny. He didn't know she was alive, but that didn't matter. It didn't stop her from daydreaming.

Today it was different because Natalie was there. Tall, slim, pretty enough so that some of the boys looked at her when they weren't busy running or yelling encouragement to their teammates. She was wearing pink shorts with a pink and white striped blouse, and her narrow feet were encased in white sandals. Pudge was stuffed into her usual old jeans, and even though Amy's jeans weren't faded, they looked sleazy beside Natalie's pink shorts.

The other two girls were seated in the bleachers. Amy climbed up to sit beside Pudge, responding with a listless "Hi" to Natalie's greeting. It was a pretty good game, but it was awkward because Amy had to go to the bathroom three times before the Blues finally won, six to four. By the last time, people were giving her dirty looks for climbing past them.

Then when they were all walking away, heading for the Dairy Queen for something to eat, Amy said, "Order me a burger and fries and a jumbo Coke, Pudge; I have to go to the bathroom."

Natalie gave her a funny look. "Again?" she asked, incredulous.

"Yes, again," Amy said defensively. "Anything wrong with that? Do I have to ask your permission?"

"No, of course not. But you go so often. Is there something wrong?"

"I just have to go, that's all. I guess I drank a lot of grape juice this morning, plus a couple of cans of pop during the game." Nobody said any more about it, but Amy was so thirsty she had a second jumbo Coke and still needed another drink when she got home. It seemed like her whole allowance this summer was being spent on food and drink, and yet she was sneaking all that food out of the kitchen. It was a miracle her mother hadn't noticed what was missing and asked about it.

She'd only been home for half an hour when Jan shouted, "They're here! Gram's here!"

They went out in the front yard when Aunt Harriet's car drove up to the curb. Amy had been afraid to see Gram, afraid that fracturing a hip would somehow have changed her, made her older, but except for the metal framed walker she needed to move around, Gram looked the same as ever.

"Hello, Amy, love. And Jan, my, you've grown two inches since I saw you last! Matt, get that little bag of mine, will you, dear?"

"Do you need help, Mother?" Mrs. Long asked.

"No, I'm doing pretty well with this thing, except for steps." Gram started toward the house, slowly, leaning on the walker bars.

Aunt Harriet, who was tall and plump, greeted the others and then looked critically at Amy. "Good grief, Irene, aren't you feeding this child? She's skin and bones!"

Mrs. Long laughed. "Bill says she runs it off with nervous energy. Heaven knows she eats enough to be twins. Here, let me take that other bag; Matt will get the rest later."

Amy followed slowly. If she'd said anything about Aunt Harriet being fat, someone would have smacked her. Why was it okay for adults to make such remarks about a kid? She couldn't help it if she was skinny.

Before she joined the others, she went into the kitchen and poured herself a big glass of grape juice, with plenty of ice.

3.

Sharing a room with Jan was even worse than she'd expected. It wasn't that her younger sister was a pest; actually, Jan was clearly trying to make Amy comfortable.

"After all," Mrs. Long had said, "she's losing her privacy, too. So do the best you can, please."

Admittedly the room was the neatest Amy had ever seen it. The floor was relatively free of clutter. The stuffed animals were on the shelves where they belonged. A section had been set aside for Amy's favorite books, the ones she'd felt she had to bring with her. Jan had promised to try to remember to make her bed before she went downstairs every morning.

But Jan was *there*. When Amy wanted to read, or to write her own stories, Jan was listening to her radio or playing tapes. When Pudge came over and they wanted to talk, they couldn't do it without being overheard. When Pudge brought out her colored pens and did sketches to illustrate Amy's stories, Jan came over and admired them and even that was an intrusion, though Pudge was pleased to have the additional approval.

Worst of all, Amy couldn't figure out how to eat or drink without her younger sister being aware of it.

The second night, she was so thirsty she gave up running to the kitchen every few minutes for a drink. She made a big pitcher of grape juice and carried it upstairs, ice cubes clinking. Jan stared at it in amazement.

"Are you going to drink *all* of that by yourself?"

Amy stifled her annoyance. "You can have some if you want it, but you'll have to go get a glass."

"I don't want any," Jan told her. "I just can't imagine anybody drinking that much in one day."

Jan made remarks about how often she went to the bathroom, too. "Every time I need to go in there, you're using it," she complained.

The matter of food was just as bad. Amy had candy bars under her pillow—smuggled upstairs past the whole family, in a way that had not been necessary when she'd been in her own room off the downstairs hall. She tried to have apples and bananas around, and Jan always smelled the bananas. And when she made sandwiches (always more than one), she tried to eat with her back turned to her sister while she was reading.

"Are you still eating that?" Jan would ask, and Amy never told her it was a different sandwich from the one Jan had seen earlier.

Pudge didn't come over the day after Gram arrived. When she called on the following day, she sounded a bit guilty.

"You didn't want to do anything energetic, you said, so I went on a hike with Natalie. Out past the golf course. Danny Crowell and Dean Boyd were caddying, and they waved at us."

Something very close to pain coursed through Amy. She didn't own Pudge, she knew that, but it hurt to see her best friend getting so friendly with a newcomer. She swallowed past that, though, and said, "Why don't you come over this afternoon and you can draw the rest of the pictures to go with my story. I finished it last night."

"Well, uh . . . Natalie invited me over to her house to hear some new tapes. She said I could bring you along."

Amy's grip tightened on the telephone receiver. "Oh. Well, no, I don't think so. We're not supposed to go away and leave Gram alone. . . ."

That was an outright lie. Gram said she could

23

get around between her bedroom—*Amy's* bedroom—and the living room all right. If someone brought her a glass of water before they went, to sit beside her chair, and left her the remote control for the TV, she could manage for hours by herself. Besides, there were three of them, Matt and Jan and herself, and it was seldom that they needed to be gone at the same time.

Amy just didn't want to be dragged along to Natalie's like an extra wheel. She stayed home and tried to write a new story, but it didn't come as easily as she was used to. She kept wondering what Pudge and Natalie were doing, if they were talking about her, if Pudge was going to drop her as a best friend and go with Natalie instead.

The very thought made Amy feel like crying.

If she hadn't been so unhappy, she'd have enjoyed Gram's company, the way she usually did. Well, she had to admit she *did* enjoy listening to Gram's tales about cooking one summer on a ranch in Montana, or going up in a hot air balloon, or seeing the ancient ruins in Athens. Gram was a travel agent now, so she got to fly to all kinds of fascinating places, but even before she took that job, she'd been an adventurer. When Dad was a kid, he'd done lots of things with Gram that Amy thought sounded very exciting.

"Does it hurt a lot to have a broken hip?" Amy asked.

Gram considered. "Well, it hurt pretty bad when I fell, and until they did the surgery and put the pin it." She held up her hands, indicating the size of the pin, eight or ten inches long. "It's stainless steel, with a bend in the top like this. Should keep me from ever breaking that hip again. It hurts some when I have to do my exercises to get that big muscle working. But I'm supposed to go on a cruise up the Inland Passage from Seattle to Alaska in the spring, and I'm determined to be well enough to go," Gram said. "So I just grit my teeth and do what I have to do to get better."

Amy was gritting her teeth over various things, too. She didn't want to move Gram out of her room, but she'd sure be glad when Gram was well enough to go home.

It felt strange, when Gram sent her to get a book, to stand in her own bedroom and see it looking as if it belonged to someone else. Gram's robe over the foot of the bed, slippers beside it. Gram's toilet things laid out on the dresser. Unfamiliar brushes and a picture of Grampa Long, who had died so many years ago that Amy only dimly remembered him, on the night table. Once again the tears prickled behind her eyelids, as they seemed to do so often these days.

When Pudge came over to ask if she wanted to go skating, Amy's spirits brightened, but not for long, for Pudge immediately added, "Natalie knows the guy who runs the rink, and he'll let us in for half price."

"Does that mean Natalie's going, too?"

"Sure. She's the one who knows the manager. She's fun, Amy. Give her a chance, and you'll like her."

But Natalie would make some remark about how often Amy had to go to the bathroom, or the fact that she drank two jumbo Cokes to everybody else's one.

"I don't guess I'll go this time," Amy said, and saw Pudge's face fall in disappointment. There was some satisfaction in that, though not much, because Pudge was going to go without her.

"Come over and spend the night tomorrow, anyway," Pudge urged. "Mom's making brownies, and we're going to have a barbecue."

It was the kind of thing Amy had enjoyed many times at the Rapinchuck house, but now she was suspicious. "Is Natalie going to be there, too?"

"No, just you and me. Come on, Amy."

"Okay," Amy agreed, and for a while she felt better.

Not for long, though.

That night the thirst was the worst it had ever been. She craved something very cold, and the grape juice was all gone, so she mixed the last of the frozen lemonade, and loaded it with ice. There was no way to hide a full pitcher, the way she'd hidden the po-

26

tato chips and a sandwich. She carried it across the hall to the stairs when the grown-ups were watching TV.

Jan commented when she came up later, "Did you drink that whole thing by yourself?" Amy ignored her.

After her sister was asleep—with a night-light on, as if she were a baby, Amy thought in disgust—Amy ate the Mars bar she'd had concealed under her pillow, being very careful not to let the wrapper crackle when she opened it. She'd have to empty the wastebasket so no one else would see how many wrappers it contained.

She woke up feeling disoriented and frightened. She'd been dreaming something horrible; someone had been chasing her and she'd been trying to find a bathroom while Natalie laughed and said, "What, again?" and then she'd fallen into a hole and gone tumbling down and down and down—

Amy suddenly came fully awake, not believing what she felt. She couldn't have wet the bed! She *couldn't* have!

But she had.

For a few moments she was so shocked she could hardly breathe. She was eleven years old, and she hadn't wet the bed ever, as far back as she could remember.

Yet her pajamas and the sheet beneath her were sopping.

For the first time she wasn't annoyed by the night-light, because otherwise she'd have had to risk waking Jan by turning on a lamp.

Amy was shaking as she stripped off her pajamas and felt around in the drawer for a clean pair. She felt practically scalded with shame. How could it have happened? She peeled the sheets off the bed and rolled them in a ball. She'd have to take them downstairs and hide them in the laundry room, hoping her mother wouldn't find them before she had a chance to wash them. Or would it be better to wash them right now? Everybody but Gram was sleeping on the second floor and wouldn't hear the washer going. There was nothing the matter with Gram's hearing, though; would she wonder, if she heard the sounds, enough to ask about it in the morning?

Amy was glad there was a night-light burning at the bottom of the stairs, too. That was for Gram, if she had to get up in the night, though of course nobody would think anything of it if she turned on lights all over the place.

She loaded the sheets in the washer, poured in detergent, and turned on the machine. Then she padded through the silent house, past Gram's door, and back up the stairs.

There were more sheets in the hall closet; she located them by feel, but didn't know what to do when she returned to the room she shared with Jan.

The mattress was wet, too. The best thing she could think of was to put some towels over the wet area and hope it wouldn't leave a spot that her mother would eventually question.

By the time she crawled into the remade bed, Amy was shivering, though it wasn't really very cold. A pair of tears squeezed their way past her tightly closed eyelids. What was wrong with her?

It was a long time before she went back to sleep.

4.

The next day was Saturday. Mr. Long went to work at his usual time, but Mrs. Long didn't. She was up early, though, before Amy could get down to put the sheets into the dryer. Would her mother wonder when she found them in the washing machine?

"Oh, Amy, there you are. Will you get me another can of juice out of the freezer and mix it up? Jan, set the table please; and when Matt comes down, tell him Joe called, will you?"

Amy went out into the utility room where the freezer was, appalled to see that there was only one can of juice left. Had she really been the one who drank most of it? She loaded the sheets into the

30

dryer and hoped her mother would think she'd left them there herself.

Matt was on the phone when she passed him in the hall; he grinned and punched her on the shoulder in a brotherly manner as she passed. "Don't eat my share of the French toast before I get there, hear? Yeah, Joe, give me half an hour, and I'll meet you there."

The family was assembled in the kitchen and there was so much noise nobody could hear the dryer running in the room next door. Amy put the orange juice in the blender and ran that, too, to add to the covering sounds. "This is the last of the juice, Mom," she said.

Mrs. Long turned from the stove with a platter of sausages, the little ones Amy liked best. "Already? Good heavens, you kids are eating us out of house and home. Somebody cleaned out the cookies, too. Why don't you girls make up another batch today? Here, let Gram get started. Jan, bring the syrup, or would you rather have apple butter, Mother?"

It was a typical morning in the Long household, except for the way Amy was feeling.

She'd wet the bed. She could imagine the way they'd all look at her if they knew. Even Pudge wouldn't understand how she could have done it.

Pudge. She was supposed to spend the night at Pudge's, after the barbecue. What if she wet the bed there?

Amy felt suddenly sick. She'd die of embarrassment if Mrs. Rapinchuck knew she wet the bed. What if the kids at school found out and they teased her? Probably Pudge wouldn't be able to take the torment and would drop her for good, and run around with Natalie instead. And Danny Crowell would *never* say "hi" to her again when they passed in the halls. Nobody would.

She stared at the French toast on her plate, the maple syrup leaking over to surround the sausages. She was still starving, and she'd been looking forward to Mr. Rapinchuck's barbecued hamburgers tonight. But she couldn't spend the night over there. She didn't dare.

"Amy?"

She realized her mother had said something to her that she hadn't heard. "I'm sorry, guess I was daydreaming."

"Sometimes you remind me so much of myself at eleven that you scare me," her mother said, laughing. "I asked if you'd go to the market for me today. There's too much to expect Dad to bring home, and he may be late, anyway. I'll make out a list. I'll give you a blank check. I have an appointment to interview the new librarian at ten, so I won't have time to shop myself."

"If you're going near the Knit Shop," Gram added, "I'll give you some money, too. Pick out the yarn you want, you and Jan, and I'll knit each one of you a sweater while I'm crippled up and can't do anything more useful."

Would Gram want to make her a sweater if she knew about last night? Amy wondered. Gram was pretty understanding, but how could anybody understand an eleven-year-old wetting the bed?

Amy cleaned up her plate, hesitated, then speared the last two sausages on the platter, since nobody else was taking them. She was the last one at the table, and she drained the juice pitcher, too.

"You want to go pick out yarn?" she asked Jan when she was ready to leave.

"No. I'm going over to Betty's; we're going to meet Donna and Alice and go skating. You pick it for me, Amy. Blue, maybe, a pretty blue, or green. Whichever you like best."

Jan was gone, off to have a good time. She didn't have to worry about people remarking on how often she went to the bathroom, Amy thought bitterly, nor be afraid to spend the night with a friend.

She rode her bike, which had a deep basket for carrying the groceries. She went to the Knit Shop first, and chose a soft blue yarn for her sister and a variegated orange, white, and brown for herself. Gram made great sweaters when she had time to knit.

By the time she reached the Easy Supermarket,

33

Amy wasn't feeling very well. Her head ached so badly she had trouble remembering where things were, though she'd been coming to this store all her life.

Juice, lots of juice, she thought dimly. She filled one end of her cart with frozen cans, mostly grape and apple.

Grace, the girl at the checkout stand, smiled at her. "Hi, Amy. My, you having a party?"

"Party?" Amy echoed stupidly. She felt terrible.

"I thought with all the juice maybe you were making punch for a party."

"Oh. No, we're just drinking lots because it's hot," Amy said. Would Grace mention it to Dad?

She'd bought so much she had trouble getting it in the basket on her bike. She had to take out the yarn and hold that bag with one hand on the handlebars.

She felt so rotten she did something she hadn't done since she was a little kid. She stepped off the curb without checking the traffic, and heard the squeal of brakes and the scream of tires on the pavement.

The bike wobbled, the top cans of grape juice fell out, and she dropped the bag of yarn.

"You stupid kid, watch what you're doing!" the driver yelled at her. His face was white. "I could have killed you!"

Amy couldn't think of anything to say in reply, since it had been stupid, and if his brakes and his reflexes hadn't been good, he might indeed have killed her.

She was shaking as she picked up the cans and the bag; the bike wobbled so badly she could hardly make it balance. What was the matter with her? Was she losing her mind now, too?

The headache was making her slightly sick to her stomach by the time she reached home. Gram and Matt were laughing over some card game they were playing and didn't pay any attention to her as she hauled her purchases into the house.

She put the groceries away and had picked up the bag with the yarn to take to Gram when it hit her.

She barely made it to the bathroom before she threw up. She'd thrown up before, when she had the flu last winter, but never like this. Her stomach hurt, her head hurt, and she was icy cold and weak and shaking, so that when the spasms were over she crouched there on the tile floor, unable to move.

Something was horribly wrong, Amy thought, and wished her mother would come.

"Amy? Hey, what's going on?"

It was Matt; he'd heard the violent eruption and come to investigate. When she looked at him, her eyes didn't seem to want to focus, and she wondered if she were going to faint. Faint? Nobody fainted these days, that was only tightly corseted ladies in old-fashioned books.

"Amy?" Matt knelt beside her, his face anxious. "You all right now?"

Her mouth tasted terrible and she wondered if she were dying, she felt so awful. "No," she said thickly. "I'm sick. Really sick, Matt."

He stared into her face, then touched her lightly on the shoulder and stood up. "Hang on. I'll get some help."

She huddled there on the floor that now seemed ice cold against her bare legs. There were goose bumps showing below her red shorts. There couldn't be anything left to come up, but she was going to throw up again.

"Amy? Honey, what's happening?" It was Gram, balancing with her walker, looking through the bathroom door.

Amy couldn't reply, once more in those violent spasms. She heard Matt's voice as if he were at the opposite end of a wind tunnel.

"She's awful sick. I don't know where to call Mom, so I'll get Dad at the store." He sounded scared.

Amy wanted to lie down and pass out. She leaned her head against the side of the bathtub, and that was cold, too, sending tremors through her.

"Gram—" Her voice was no more than a squawk. "I think I'm going to die."

"Dad's not at the store, he went somewhere—" Matt's voice went up and down, as if someone were fiddling with the volume control on the TV. "What'll I do?"

Gram made the decision. "This is more than a simple upset stomach. Call an ambulance," she said.

And ten minutes later two young men in white pants and navy blue shirts were lifting Amy off the bathroom floor onto a gurney, or wheeled stretcher, covering her with a sheet, and fastening straps across her middle.

"Up you go," one of them said gently, and Amy had a dizzying view of the ceilings as she was carried out of the house, across the lawn, and put into an ambulance.

"Mom," Amy croaked.

"I'll keep trying on the phone until I get your parents," Gram said. "You go with her, Matt, so she's not alone."

One of the young men was putting a blood pressure cuff around her arm and pumping it up, the same one who'd checked her pulse before they'd put her on the stretcher.

It was hard to speak, and she still felt awful. "Am I going to die?" She had to know, had to force the words out.

37

The young man gave her a smile. "Not if I can help it, young lady. Just relax, okay? We'll take care of you."

She heard the siren and saw Matt's white face—whiter than that of the motorist who had almost run her down—and had a single coherent thought: riding in an ambulance wasn't nearly as exciting as she'd always thought it would be.

5.

There was no hospital in Marysville. The ambulance took her to the larger town of Everett, six miles away. It didn't take very long to get there.

Amy had been in the Emergency Room once before, when she'd taken a spill off her bike and gashed her knee so it needed four stitches. That time Dad had carried her in, and she'd been crying because it really hurt and it was bleeding so badly.

This time she felt too rotten to notice details. There were bright lights overhead that hurt her eyes, so she closed them. Cool fingers again checked her pulse; another blood pressure cuff was placed around her arm. Still sounding as if it came from far away was Matt's voice, answering questions.

"Who's your doctor?"

"Dr. Rosenbaum."

"You're her brother? What's her name?"

"Amy Jane Long. She's eleven."

"What happened to her? How long ago?"

Matt's answers didn't really seem to have anything to do with her. Amy drifted in a sort of haze that wasn't entirely black; through her eyelids she could tell the big light was still on directly overhead.

"Mom'll have the insurance card when she gets here," Matt was saying. "My grandmother's trying to reach her; she was interviewing somebody this morning."

"Amy?" said someone very near at hand. "We're going to take some blood to use for tests. You'll feel just a prick."

There was a cold sensation on her arm, then the needle went in. Amy didn't open her eyes. She wondered if she really *was* dying. For some reason, the thought didn't frighten her quite as much as it had when she'd collapsed on the floor in the bathroom. There were people surrounding her, taking care of things. The man in the ambulance had said she wasn't going to die if he could help it.

There was one clear thought before the haze got thicker and took over completely. Now she wouldn't have to worry about explaining to Pudge why she couldn't stay overnight.

How long did she drift? She felt hands touching

her, felt cold and someone covered her with a blanket (had she said she was cold?), and wanted a drink worse than she'd ever wanted one in her life.

A familiar voice struck through the haze as a warm hand touched her bare arm. "Amy? It's Dr. Rosenbaum."

She sighed, glad he was here. He'd taken care of her since she was a baby; he'd help her now.

Matt was explaining all over again while the doctor examined her, lifting an eyelid to look at her eyes, probing her stomach.

"That hurt? Or that?"

Amy muttered something unintelligible.

"She was so sick," Matt said. "She threw up gallons, it looked like to me, and then she couldn't stand up or anything."

"What did she have to eat last?"

"She had French toast and sausage at breakfast with the rest of us. And juice. Orange juice."

"Syrup on the toast?"

"Yeah," Matt said. He sounded more scared than Amy was. "She . . . she's been kind of . . . funny for the last week or so, I guess. She's been drinking an awful lot, and I've heard her going to the bathroom in the middle of the night. She never used to do that. Come to think of it, she's been spending a lot of time in the bathroom during the day, too. And she's been too tired to run with me. Is she . . . is she going to be okay?"

41

"I'll tell you more after we do a few tests," Dr. Rosenbaum said. "She's pretty dehydrated. Let's get an IV going. Tell you what, you go out in the waiting room and try again to reach your mom and dad, all right?"

Amy liked the touch of the warm, gentle hand that now rested reassuringly on her shoulder. Only she wished her parents would come.

She seemed to be floating in and out of reality. Hands touched her, someone sponged her arm in the crook of her elbow with something cold, and a voice said softly, "This is going to prick a little, Amy."

After that, she thought maybe she slept a little or something. Nobody did anything to her for a while, anyway.

And then she heard her mother's voice. "Amy? Honey, how are you? Can you hear me?"

She struggled to get her eyes open against the weight that wanted to hold them shut. She saw her mother's stricken face, felt the warm embrace as Mrs. Long bent over her, glimpsed her dad looking just as alarmed, and felt hot tears brim over as she re-closed her eyes against the light that was too bright.

She listened to the voices, her mother's quickened with anxiety, her father's deeper but just as urgent.

"A bad case of the flu?" he was asking.

"Maybe. We're waiting for the lab results," Dr. Rosenbaum said. "Ah, here we are now . . ." His voice trailed off. Amy heard the voices, but it was as if none of what they said had anything to do with her.

Beside her, Amy heard Dr. Rosenbaum exhale audibly. "That's it, then. It's diabetes."

"Diabetes." Mrs. Long repeated the word, choking on it, letting go of Amy's hand, then grabbing it again, hard.

Diabetes. Amy thought she'd heard the word, but she couldn't remember when, or what it meant. The doctor's voice came very close to her ear.

"Amy, you've been going to the bathroom a lot lately, the way Matt said? Drinking a lot of water?"

It was an effort to form the words to reply. "Grape juice," she said, trying to be factual.

She heard her mother say, "Oh, my God," in a despairing sort of way, and then, as she later described it to Pudge, Amy sort of went away. The voices grew softer until she couldn't understand them anymore, and she no longer felt sick, just very tired, and she wasn't even aware of the big bright light overhead.

She woke up in a hospital room.

It had pale yellow walls and there was a mural directly opposite the bed that looked vaguely familiar. After a few moments she recognized it from one of Jan's Serendipity books: the fat furry creature her sister had referred to as "that guy who cleaned up the dirty castle" so the Grunk wouldn't eat him and his friends. She couldn't think of his name yet, and for some reason it seemed important. Oh yeah, Bangalee.

Amy shifted position and felt something pull in her left arm. A plastic tube was taped in place at the crook of her elbow, connected to a bottle of clear liquid on a stand beside the bed. She'd seen enough hospital shows to know it was called an IV. Something was running from the bottle into her arm.

She felt confused and scared as memory returned. She'd gotten terribly sick and Matt had called an ambulance, and the man had said she wasn't going to die if he could help it.

Well, she hadn't died, obviously. The memories of the Emergency Room were dim, for the most part. Had her family gone home and left her here? she wondered.

"Amy? Are you awake?"

"Mom?" She turned her head toward the door and saw her parents coming in. Mrs. Long's eyes looked as if she'd been crying.

"Hi, honey. How you feeling?"

"I don't know. Tired. Awful tired. And my stomach's sore." Amy glanced toward the windows. "Is it afternoon? I'll have to tell Pudge I can't go to the barbecue."

"That was last night, honey. We already told her. It's Sunday morning."

It made Amy feel peculiar to hear that all of yesterday afternoon and evening were gone, and she didn't even know what had happened to most of it.

"What's the matter with me? Have I got the flu again, only worse?"

She saw her mother's lips tremble, her eyes fill with tears, and Amy felt the dread growing within her. Not the flu. What had Dr. Rosenbaum said to them? She couldn't quite remember.

Her father drew up two chairs beside the bed and without waiting for his wife to sit down took a seat himself and reached for Amy's hand.

"It's not the flu, Amy. You have something called diabetes."

She stared into his face. "What's that?"

"It . . . it's what happens to people when their pancreas doesn't work right and it stops producing something called insulin. The nurse here, Mr. Soldenski, will be explaining it to you; it's kind of complicated."

Diabetes. That's what Dr. Rosenbaum had said. She remembered now.

"How did I catch it?" Amy wanted to know.

Her father cleared his throat. "You don't catch it. Actually, they don't know yet why some people get it and some don't. It's genetic, that means it runs in families, but I guess it's not always hereditary."

His hand was squeezing hers so tightly that it was

a bit uncomfortable. "Now they think that sometimes diabetes might be caused by a virus—similar to the flu. Matt says you've been drinking a lot, going to the bathroom more often, for weeks. And eating more."

Mrs. Long tried to smile. "We knew you were eating a lot, but that's not so unusual for kids. When they're growing fast, they need a lot of food."

Except that she wasn't growing fast, Amy thought. Hadn't her mother noticed that she'd hardly grown at all this summer, that she hadn't needed any new clothes in a larger size, like Jan and Matt?

"I don't feel as sick today," Amy said.

"That's because they're giving you insulin," her dad told her. "You should feel a lot better soon, and then we'll take you home."

Amy nodded. "Good. How long will it take to get over the diabetes?"

There was no mistaking it. The tears shimmered in her mother's eyes, and Mrs. Long groped for a handkerchief. Mr. Long cleared his throat again, and his voice was husky.

"You don't get over diabetes, Amy," he said gently. "Once you have it, you have it for the rest of your life."

6.

Amy felt as if her mouth was filled with cotton that had absorbed all the moisture, and her heart had begun to pound. She was aware that the headache was coming back, too.

"You mean I'm going to be sick forever?"

Mrs. Long bit her lip and turned her head, frightening Amy very much. It was Mr. Long who answered.

"They can't cure diabetes yet, though maybe they will during your lifetime. They can control it, though. Mr. Soldenski will be teaching you what you'll have to do."

Amy's lips were stiff so the words were hard to form. "Like what? Am I going to have to stay in bed all my life?" And keep throwing up, she wanted to cry out, and wet the bed so I can't ever go anywhere again?

"Well, the first thing they'll teach us about—your mom and I have to learn quite a bit, too—is diet. Diabetics have to have the right balance of foods, among carbohydrates, fats, and proteins, so you'll have to pay more attention to what you eat. With diabetes you can't handle sugar the way other people do, so you'll have to be careful about that."

"No sugar?" Amy was incredulous. She thought of the Milky Way hidden under her pillow at home, waiting for her to get it. Or had her mother already found it and taken it away?

"I talked to the dietician this morning," her mother said, making a valiant effort to keep her voice level. "She said mostly you'll have to give up candy and cakes, except those made with sugar substitutes, or keep them to very small servings. Chocolate, things like that. You'll probably be able to have ice cream or sherbet occasionally, when they get your condition under control."

"No chocolate? You mean I'm *never* going to be able to have chocolate again?" Amy heard her voice rising and swallowed hard.

"Look, honey, don't worry about it. We'll work it out when Mom understands what we have to do. The main thing is that you're going to be okay."

Okay? Amy wondered. She felt numb. How could she be okay if she couldn't eat chocolate or sugar?

"Will I have to take medicine?"

Her parents exchanged a meaningful glance, and Amy braced herself. "Something horrid tasting?"

Her father was having a terrible time with his throat, and he couldn't seem to let go of her hand. "Well, the only medicine for diabetes is insulin, and you can't take that by mouth. They have to give it to you in shots."

"Shots?" Amy hated shots. She'd had a tetanus injection when she'd gashed her knee. "How often will I have to have shots?"

It wasn't reassuring to see that her mother was incapable of answering. Again it was Mr. Long who told her. "They don't know for sure yet, but probably twice a day, to start with."

"Two shots? Every day?" She couldn't believe it. She didn't want to believe it. Except, when she looked at her mother, she had to.

Pudge came to see her right after lunch, bringing a new book from the library. "I didn't read it yet," she said nervously, glancing around the hospital room. "I thought you'd like it first."

"I'm sorry I missed the barbecue," Amy said.

"Yeah. We missed you. Dad said to tell you we'll have a special one for you when you come home." She cleared her throat, just the way Mr. Long kept doing when he talked to Amy. "Do you know how long you'll have to be here?"

"Not yet. They said usually not more than three or four days." She wanted to ask if Natalie had gone to the barbecue and spent the night, but she wasn't sure she really wanted to know, if she had. "I have to learn how to give myself shots, Mr. Soldenski said."

Pudge turned pale. "Your mom said you'd have to have shots; she didn't say you'd have to give them to yourself. How gross!"

"For the rest of my life," Amy said. "And I have to learn a lot of stuff about what I can eat, and what I can't. Can't is like candy bars and cake and cookies. I don't know yet what that leaves."

"Geeze!" Pudge put the book down on the nightstand. "What's that stuff that's going into your arm? Does it hurt?"

"Not really. Not unless I forget and move too far and the tube pulls where it goes in. It's something to replace all the fluids I lost when I threw up and had to go to the bathroom so often."

"Natalie said there must be something wrong with you, that you had to go so much. Listen, do you think you'll be well in time to go to school?"

"I don't know. I hope so. In a little while Mr. Soldenski starts teaching me what I have to do about everything. He's the nurse in the pediatrics ward who does the teaching." She'd learned a few new words since she'd been here.

"He's a man, and he's a nurse? I thought nurses were women!" Pudge said, sitting gingerly on the edge of a chair.

"He's a nurse, and there's a woman doctor, so I guess you can be either one. He's sort of nice, I guess. If he wasn't going to make me give myself shots."

"Is he young?" Pudge asked, brightening. She would be more comfortable talking about an attractive male than about medical matters. "Is he cute?"

"I guess he's young. About like Coach Framingham." The new coach at the junior high was so good-looking that all the girls wished they could have him for P.E. instead of Miss Jernigan, who looked like a stick wearing blue shorts. "And he's cute, too. He has dark curly hair and very blue eyes, and a thick mustache."

"Ooo," Pudge said. "I love mustaches."

They talked for a few minutes, and then Pudge said she had to leave. "We're going to my aunt's for dinner," she said. "I'll come back to see you tomorrow, okay?"

It was quiet when Pudge had gone. Somewhere down the hall a baby cried, and then was still. Amy wondered if babies had diabetes, too. Poor little babies, having to have shots every day. They wouldn't understand why. At least she was old enough to understand that much.

She didn't know why it had happened to her, though. How come Jan and Matt and her mother and dad were all right, and only she had diabetes?

Miss Morrison, one of the nurses, stuck her head around the edge of the door, smiling. "How you doing, Amy?"

"Okay, I guess." As well as anybody could be, Amy thought, when she'd been told she was going to have diabetes all her life, and have to take shots, and never have anything sweet to eat again.

"We're going to bring you a roommate," Miss Morrison said. "The place is filling up, so we're asking you to share. Her name's Ginny, and she's the same age you are."

"Does she have diabetes, too?"

"Yes. She's had it for about two years. You'll like her."

Amy's heart sank. "You mean she's still sick enough to be in the hospital after two years?"

"Not usually. She got lost in the woods overnight and missed her insulin shots, and she'll just be here long enough to get it regulated again and for observation; she got sort of scratched up while she was wandering around on the mountainside."

Amy had mixed feelings about having company. She rather liked the privacy, though there wasn't anything she was doing—or *could* do—that made being alone important. On the other hand, it was boring with nothing to do but watch TV on the set suspended from the ceiling. Soap operas and game shows didn't interest her much.

Ginny didn't arrive on a stretcher, the way Amy knew that she had done. Ginny rode in a wheelchair, though as soon as Miss Morrison stopped pushing it, Ginny stood up and started taking off her shirt. The nurse pulled a curtain around her, then pushed it back into place against the wall when Ginny had gotten into bed, wearing one of the white gowns with blue dots on it, just like Amy.

"Ginny, this is Amy. She's a newly diagnosed diabetic. Amy, this is Ginny. Get acquainted, girls."

Amy stared at the newcomer. She was sturdier than Amy, and probably a little taller, too. She had brown hair and gray eyes, and while she wasn't pretty she looked pleasant and friendly. There was a big scratch across one cheek, and another one on her neck.

Ginny said, "Hi."

"Hi," Amy responded. "I heard you got lost. It must have been scary, being alone all night in the woods."

"Well, it was, sort of. I knew enough not to walk in circles. I waited by a creek where there was water to drink, after I'd plowed through some bushes trying to find a path. I got leaves and pine boughs to fix a place to sleep where I wouldn't get too cold."

"Did you get really sick?" Amy imagined being as sick as she had been yesterday, alone all night, without any help.

"Not really," Ginny said matter-of-factly. "I got pretty hungry, and I'd have liked something to drink besides creek water. I had a few Life Savers with me, but no insulin. I'm supposed to carry my supply pouch with me, but my dad had it, and we got separated when I stopped to look at some funny toadstool things. I was real glad when I heard the searchers yelling for me this morning."

"Do you give your own shots?" Amy asked. She still couldn't quite believe that anybody expected kids to stick needles into themselves.

"Sure. I have since I was nine. Have you done it yet?"

"No. I'm going to learn tomorrow."

"Nothing to it," Ginny said surprisingly. "I'd rather give myself the shots than stick my fingers for the blood tests."

Amy's heart lurched. Was there no end to the horrible surprises?

"You mean there's something worse than the shots?"

"I thought so when I first learned how to take care of myself. None of it bothers me much any more. You get used to it."

I won't get used to it, Amy thought angrily. I'll never, never get used to it.

54

And then she wondered what would happen if she didn't do the things they told her, if she refused to give shots and stick her finger to make it bleed for a test, and if she ate candy bars. What would happen then?

7.

It seemed odd to have a male nurse; Amy had always thought of nurses as being females. She would have liked him instantly if she hadn't been so apprehensive about what he was going to do.

"I'm not on a regular shift, like your floor nurses," he told her. "I come in when I'm needed. I'll be helping you learn how to handle your diabetes, and even after you go home, you can call me if you want to."

Amy felt frozen, unable to respond.

"Most of the kids call me Ed," Mr. Soldenski said. "When they aren't calling me something worse because I'm always sticking needles in them."

He grinned when a voice behind him said, "Yeah,

56

old Vampire Soldenski. Can't live without taking a gallon of blood from each one of us every day."

Mr. Soldenski was still grinning. "I've told you a million times, Coby, not to exaggerate. I never take more than a quart from any one patient in any twenty-four hour period. You young ladies met Coby Bonner yet?"

"Hi, Coby," Ginny greeted the boy who was slouched in the doorway. He was older than they were, maybe thirteen or fourteen, and unlike Mr. Soldenski he didn't look like a movie star. In fact, Coby was one of the homeliest boys Amy had ever seen. He had a big nose, and his brown hair was badly cut and needed to be combed. He wore old blue jeans and a faded blue shirt; there was a silver-colored chain around his neck with some kind of tag on it, which Amy couldn't make out from across the room. Coby didn't look the type to wear jewelry, she thought.

"Hi, Ginny. When do I get to break out of this joint?" Coby addressed the nurse who was standing at the foot of Ginny's bed.

"In an awful hurry, aren't you? You just got here. Your mom and your doctor think we ought to run you through a refresher course on diabetes, so maybe some of it will stick this time and you won't be back again so often." Mr. Soldenski was still smiling, and his voice was pleasant, but there was an underlying seriousness in his words.

Coby shrugged. "So run it by me again. I gotta break out of here by tomorrow morning, at the latest. I got a ball game to play at one o'clock tomorrow."

"How's the team doing? How's your batting average holding up?"

"We're in second place. And"—Coby's rather ugly face split in a grin that made him, for an instant, almost attractive—"they ain't gonna get to first place without me." He went through the motions of swinging an imaginary bat with great force. "Home Run King of the Summer League, that's what they call me."

Ed Soldenski gestured toward Amy with one hand. "You met Amy yet?"

The gray eyes that settled on her were surprisingly sharp. Amy had the feeling that they noticed everything, from the hair that needed washing to the number of freckles across her nose. "Hi," she said uncertainly.

"Hi, Amy. You one of us?"

"Us?" she echoed, not understanding.

"Yeah. You know," Coby said, sauntering into the room and thrusting toward her the tag on the chain around his neck. "A sugar baby. A good shot of sugar makes babies of us all, right, Ed?"

The words on the tag jumped out at Amy at close range. They said I AM A DIABETIC.

"Well, some of the things we do make us seem rather infantile," Ed Soldenski amended.

58

Something about the way he'd spoken, and suddenly spotting a chain similar to Coby's around his neck, brought Amy's question out without thinking. "Are *you* diabetic, too?"

"That's right," the R.N. said easily. "Only I'm a Type II, and you kids are all Type I."

Amy, bewildered, only stared at him.

"That's right, you haven't heard about all this yet, have you? Well, Type II diabetics—"

"Oh, crap," Coby said, "you pushed his button. Now he starts with the lectures."

The nurse went on as if he hadn't been interrupted. "—usually get diabetes as adults, and they've often been overweight. Believe it or not, I weighed over a hundred pounds more than I do now when I was diagnosed, and that's probably part of the reason my diabetes came on when it did."

Amy looked at him: so healthy, so good-looking, in such high spirits all the time, at least since she'd been here. "You mean you have to take shots, too?"

"No, that's why he can laugh about sucking our blood," Coby said. "He don't have to get stuck himself."

"Type IIs, or non-insulin dependent diabetics," Ed said, ignoring Coby, "can often control their diabetes with diet and exercise. So I went on a diet, lost one hundred and twelve pounds, and run ten miles a day, and that keeps my blood sugars within reasonable limits, though I have to check it all the time the same as you do. Now, you kids are all Type I. That means your own pancreas isn't producing any insulin, so we have to give it to you with shots. You're what we call insulin dependent, because you can't live without that insulin."

Well, Amy thought, feeling cold, she guessed that answered her question about what happened if she refused to take the shots.

"We're going to meet down in the Peds lounge in an hour," Ed Soldenski said. "That IV is finished, we can unhook you now, Amy. You girls can get dressed in your own clothes if you feel like it. Ginny, you show Amy where to go, okay?"

"Sure," Ginny agreed. "I'm definitely getting dressed. I'm not traipsing around in this outfit with the back flopping open."

"Come on, Coby, you can help me set up," Ed said, slapping a hand on Coby's shoulder.

"Oh, crumb, not that stupid puppet show again!" Coby protested as he was guided out of the room. "Have a heart! If I have to see that thing one more time, I'm gonna puke!"

Amy was feeling confused; she hadn't understood half of what she'd just heard. She fastened on one of the last things. "What's the . . . the 'peed's' lounge?" she asked.

Ginny thumped her pillow into a more comfortable position. "Pediatrics lounge. We're in the pediatrics ward, that means for kids. And the lounge is

60

just where we can go when we're ambulatory—that means able to walk around. It's like a living room, with a TV and couches and some games, stuff like that."

"You've been here before, I guess. Lots of times." Amy sounded hollow, and that was sort of the way she felt. Was the whole rest of her life going to be like this, in and out of the hospital every little while?

"Well, I was here five days when I first got diabetes," Ginny agreed. "They couldn't figure out what was the matter with me at first. They thought I had the flu real bad, because I kept throwing up and like that, and I got dehydrated from losing all the fluids, and I couldn't keep anything down. So they put me in here and hooked me up to an IV to get fluids back into me. They still thought I had the flu, because I didn't test out for any kind of infection and I kept on being sick. And then one day Ed came in and stopped with a funny look on his face, and came across to my bed and said, 'Ginny, blow in my face.' I did, and he pulled back and said, 'Your breath's bad.' Before I had a chance to feel insulted, he said, 'Maybe that's a clue to what's wrong with you. I think you may be acidotic. Let's get another test and find out.' The next thing I knew they were stabbing me for more blood, and everybody was all excited because they'd found out I was diabetic."

Amy was bewildered. "It seems like a funny thing to be happy about."

Ginny shrugged. "Well, it meant they knew what was the matter with me, and what to do about it. What do you think about Coby?"

"Think about him? I don't know. He's sort of . . . smart-mouthed, I guess. He doesn't act sick."

"He wouldn't be, if he ate the way he's supposed to, and took his insulin when he should. He goes to my school," Ginny said. "He misses a lot. The reason he knows Ed so well is that he's in here quite often. I don't think anybody at home cares enough about him to remind him, the way my folks do. Boy, my folks ask me all the time, 'Virginia, have you had your insulin?' At Coby's he's alone most of the time, I guess, and maybe he doesn't care if he does what he's supposed to or not."

"Do you think it's true that Mr. Soldenski—Ed—was really fat once?"

"Oh, sure. I've seen pictures of him. He wasn't even cute when he was so fat, but he sure is now, isn't he?" Ginny sighed. "He's got a girl friend. Miss Orton. She's a nurse down in the maternity section. She takes care of newborn babies. You want to get dressed and go down and see the babies before we meet in the lounge?"

"Will they let us?" Amy was already sitting up, perched on the edge of the high bed. Anything seemed better than lying here doing nothing, and she *did* feel a lot better.

"Sure. We have to look at the babies through a window, of course. They're really cute."

Amy's mother had brought her fresh clothes, and she got dressed in jeans and a yellow shirt and sandals. It felt a bit strange to be walking again, but she decided it was safe enough; she wasn't going to fall down. She half expected someone to say something when they left their room, but the nurses at the station outside only looked up and smiled, so she guessed it was okay.

Ginny knew her way around. They took an elevator up one floor and followed the signs to the maternity ward. There were six babies beyond the big window, wrapped in pink or blue blankets, each in a tiny bassinet. Two of them had heavy, dark hair, one of them had soft blonde wisps, and the rest were practically bald.

"Four girls and two boys," Ginny said, reading the cards at the foot of each bassinet. "There's another one over there in the incubator. It must be a preemie."

A preemie, Amy knew, meant a baby that had been born earlier than it should have been; it was usually very small, and maybe needed oxygen and extra heat, and the nurses kept a closer eye on it. She would like to have seen this preemie up close, but the incubator was too far away, across the room.

On their way back to "peeds" as Ginny called their floor, Amy said, "I didn't understand half what the rest of you were talking about a while ago. What was it you said Ed thought when he smelled your breath?"

"Acidotic. I mean, he thought I was in ketosis. He'll explain all that when he goes through the material. It's complicated."

"So complicated I don't know if I'll ever figure it out. What if you don't know what to do? What if you make a mistake? Will you die?"

"I guess you would if you kept on doing the wrong things," Ginny said, but she didn't sound concerned about it. "They won't let you do that, though. And once you get the hang of it, it's pretty easy. Come on, let's get a couple of suckers and go down to the lounge."

"A sucker? I thought we weren't supposed to have candy."

"These are diabetic candy. At first I didn't think they tasted as good as regular ones, but you get used to them. They're sweetened with sorbitol instead of sugar. You don't have these too often, either, though, because too many of them may make you have diarrhea."

Amy wondered how long it would take her to be able to laugh at things like that, the way Ginny did.

The suckers were on the counter at the nurses' station. They each took one, and Amy thought they tasted fine. Hers was grape flavored.

She liked Ginny, and she was glad she wasn't going into that lounge by herself, that she'd have a friend there with her.

As they walked through the doorway to the lounge, Amy felt the tightness begin in her stomach as she braced herself for the next step in this nightmare she'd fallen into.

8.

There were four other kids in the room besides Coby, who sprawled in a big chair at one side of the fake fireplace. He didn't pay any attention to them.

Amy followed Ginny over to sit on a long couch. There was already a timid-looking little boy of about seven sitting there; he looked up at Amy uncertainly, and she managed to smile at him.

When Ed came in, he introduced everybody. The little boy beside Amy was Ben. A red-headed boy who'd chosen to sit on the floor (he reminded her of Danny Crowell) was Zack; he was nine. Elizabeth, a tall girl even skinnier than Amy, was twelve; Joan was fourteen and sulky-looking, though maybe that was because she'd just been as sick as Amy had.

At the front of the room was a miniature puppet theater with red curtains. When Ed stood up beside it, Coby groaned.

"Here we go again. Idiot city," he said.

Ed gave him a pleasant smile. "Be quiet, Coby. We know you've already heard this—"

"A hundred times," Coby agreed.

"—but the rest of the kids, except for Ginny, haven't. And they need to know what's happening to them. They've all been sick, and now they need to learn why. And then we'll talk about how they're going to get better."

Ed pulled out a diagram and put it up on a display board. "Okay," he said, "let's show you what's been happening to you. This is your body, and I'm sure you recognize some of these parts. This one, for instance, is your heart; it pumps the blood through your body. You all know about your heart. And you know what the stomach does; it's where your food goes to be digested. Most of you probably don't know what this is, though." He used a stick to tap on a peculiarly shaped organ partly hidden behind the stomach. "This is your pancreas."

Coby reached over and picked up a blue and white dotted pillow, shaped the same as the organ Ed was pointing out on the chart, and waved it over his head. It was covered with red buttons.

"Yes, this is what it looks like," Ed agreed, "except

that it isn't really blue with white dots, and it doesn't have red buttons on it. What it does have, what those red buttons represent, are the cells that produce insulin. They're called the islets of Langerhans, after the doctor who discovered them. To understand what that insulin does, we'll take a closer look at the diagram."

Coby tossed the pancreas pillow, and it landed in Amy's lap.

Startled, she looked at him, but Coby was watching Ed, now. It made her feel funny to be holding the pancreas, almost as if it were the real organ that had somehow made her sick. Beside her, Ben reached out and touched one of the red buttons, then looked up at her. She could tell that Ben understood even less than she did about this.

Coby was a ballplayer, she thought. He could throw an object and have it land anywhere he wanted. So why had he picked her to throw it to? Amy returned her attention to Ed, resting the pancreas pillow on the sofa between herself and Ben.

"You all know that the food you eat is the fuel that runs your body, right? If you didn't eat, you'd starve to death. Well, it isn't as simple as just putting the food into your stomach. Everything you eat has to be changed into a form that can be used by each of the cells that make up your body," Ed said. Everybody except Coby stared at the brightly colored cartoon-type body in the picture on the display board. "The form some of it takes is glucose, which is another name for sugar. Some people think you get diabetes because you eat a lot of sugar, but that's not so. All the carbohydrates, like fruits and vegetables and the grains in bread and cereals, turn into glucose before your bloodstream can carry it to the cells to feed them."

Amy had felt a surge of guilt when he mentioned eating sugar; it subsided when he said she hadn't caused her own diabetes because of the candy bars and the cookies.

"Looks easy, doesn't it?" Ed was pointing with a stick. "You put the food in here, it goes to your stomach, turns into glucose, and travels to where it's needed. There's one more tricky step, though. Each one of those hundreds of tiny cells is like a locked room. And what do we need to get into a locked room?"

There was an embarrassed silence, and then Elizabeth said hesitantly, "A key?"

"That's right. A key. Only in this case it isn't metal, and you can't carry it in your pocket to use when you need it. The key to letting that glucose, or food, into the hungry cells is a substance called insulin. And that's when we get to here, to this funny-looking organ behind your stomach. The pancreas. Throw me the pancreas, Amy."

Self-consciously, Amy tossed him the pillow with the red buttons on it. To her relief it went all the way, and Ed caught it in one hand.

"Okay. Now, on this pancreas are the islets that produce insulin. They don't really look like red buttons, but we made them that way so you can see what happens. Each one of those islets makes some insulin that goes down here"—he demonstrated with the pointer—"and joins the glucose in the blood-stream. When the blood reaches a cell, the insulin unlocks the cell so the food can go inside and feed it. Now."

He dropped the pillow behind the puppet theater and brought forth another pillow almost like the first one. "You see what's different about this pancreas?"

Ben squirmed beside Amy on the couch. "It doesn't have any red buttons on it."

"No buttons. That means it doesn't have any islets. And if there are no islets, what do you think happens?"

This time Amy was brave enough to answer, hoping she was right. "It doesn't make any insulin."

"Exactly. And when it doesn't make any insulin, or keys to unlock the cells, what do you suppose happens to the food that is supposed to be keeping you alive and healthy?"

Nobody said anything. Ed turned to Coby, who was cleaning his fingernails with a toothpick. "Want to tell them, Coby? Just to prove you paid attention in one of the earlier sessions?"

Coby shrugged, but he dropped the toothpick in his shirt pocket. "The food can't get into the cells. It goes on past and builds up glucose, or sugar, in your blood. It makes you sick. It makes you thirsty and you have to pee all the time, and you're starving, so you eat and eat, but it doesn't do any good."

His choice of words embarrassed Elizabeth and Amy, but Ed didn't seem perturbed. "That's about it. The sugar, or glucose, builds up here, in the blood-stream. That's why we do blood testing, to tell if there's too much sugar in it, which is making you sick, or will make you sick eventually if we don't do something about it. Testing the urine was the way we used to tell how high a person's blood sugar was. Now we have a better way, and we'll talk more about that in a minute. For now let's think about what's happening here. You're eating a lot, and it's all turning to glucose the way it's supposed to, but you don't have a key to open the cells, so the food isn't keeping you from starving."

Joan spoke for the first time. "I think it all sounds disgusting," she said, and there was a tremor in her voice.

"Disgusting? Well, some people," Ed told her with a smile, "think the way the body works is quite miraculous and totally fascinating. When it's working properly, we don't give much thought to how

71

it works. We just go along enjoying ourselves. But when something goes wrong—and in the case of diabetes we don't even know for sure, yet, exactly *why* it goes wrong—we try to find a way to fix the problem. Up to about sixty years ago, when anybody got diabetes they usually died within a couple of months, because nobody knew how to help them. And then in 1922 two Canadian doctors by the names of Banting and Best discovered how to make insulin for people who couldn't produce their own."

Ed used the pointer to show them on the chart. "Once insulin is given to you to replace what your pancreas can no longer make, the cells open. They take in the food, the glucose in your bloodstream drops because it's going to feed the cells the way it's supposed to, and you start to feel better. You gain weight, and get taller, if you're growing children. Now, before I talk any more, I'm going to put on this little play for you, about a boy who gets diabetes. Seeing the puppets may help you get all this straight in your minds, okay?"

Coby made a rude noise. "Baby stuff," he said.

Ed ignored him and retreated behind the puppet theater. A moment later the red curtains parted, and the play began, concerning two boys, one with diabetes.

It was sort of a babyish play, Amy thought. But in a way she was glad to be seeing it, because it made things easier to understand. Tom, the boy with diabetes, felt the same way she did about things. He had gotten short-tempered and hard to get along with; he struck out at the people around him for little or no reason, the way she'd been doing with Jan. He was embarrassed because he had to drink so much and go to the bathroom so often. He even wet the bed and was too ashamed to tell his best friend, Bob. Amy slid a glance sideways at the other kids. Elizabeth looked pale; Joan had red spots in her cheeks. Was Joan annoyed because this was disgusting, or had she, too, experienced these humiliating things?

In the play, Tom was upset about having shots, and he worried about being too sick to be on a skating team. He talked to his friend Bob about it at last, and then Bob talked to a nurse who explained all the things Ed had just been telling them. When Tom took his shots, he'd be able to skate and play ball and do all the other things he liked to do. His disposition would improve, too, and he wouldn't have to worry about finding a bathroom so often.

The play had a happy ending, with Tom deciding that as long as he did what the doctor told him, he'd be fine. Before Ed came out from behind the puppet theater, as the curtains shut, Coby said, "See? What'd I tell you? Stupid."

Nobody else said anything. Amy couldn't tell if they thought it was stupid or not. At least it did make her understand that what was happening to

73

her wasn't her fault, and that there was something she could do about it, and that other kids had it happen to them, too.

"Now," Ed said, "we'll talk about what happens next, after we learn we have diabetes. How we get on with the rest of our lives."

Beside Amy, Ben squirmed. Then he piped up, "I have to go to the bathroom first."

Everybody laughed, even Coby and Ed.

"Okay, we'll take a ten-minute break," Ed agreed.

Amy was glad to move around for a few minutes. She stood up, then hesitated. Coby was moving toward her, the Tom puppet on one hand.

In a high-pitched voice he said, wiggling the puppet, "I don't know why I have to act in such a stupid play. I don't really like shots, nor sticking my finger for blood tests. And I *love* chocolate bars!"

Behind him Ed picked up the other puppet, also altering his voice. "But not enough to make yourself sick for the rest of your life, I hope! Not when you can feel so *great* if you do what you're supposed to!"

Coby turned and made his puppet whack the other one. "You're an idiot! You're stupid! You never lived in the real world at all!"

Ed's puppet didn't hit back. For a moment Amy thought Ed was going to say something sharp, like telling Coby to be quiet or leave. But he didn't. He stood looking at the boy with a gentle smile.

"Come back in ten minutes, Coby," he said. "I need you to help me finish this up, okay? Now, let's everybody have a diet pop out of the machine, my treat, and then we'll have to wind this up in an hour or less so we can all go to the bathroom again, right?"

Everybody laughed, including Coby, who allowed Ed to retrieve the puppet and drop it back into the miniature theater.

How could she be laughing? Amy wondered. As if she didn't have diabetes, as if she were a normal person who didn't have to worry about how she was going to get through the rest of her life taking shots every day and never having candy bars again.

Elizabeth, she saw, had tears in her eyes. Was she thinking the same things?

"Come on," Amy said softly. "Let's go have our diet pop. Maybe it won't be too bad."

"When you get used to it," Ginny said, "you don't notice the difference."

Amy followed her along the corridor, hoping that Ginny was right.

9.

The first few sips of the diet pop didn't taste quite the way her usual favorite did, but after a few more swallows Amy decided it wasn't bad. "I suppose I can live with this," she said to no one in particular.

They'd all carried their pop cans back to the Peds lounge. Joan gave her a bitter look, but it was Coby who said, in a mocking tone, "Yeah, but can you live without chocolate bars?"

Ed was setting up a new display on a low table. "There's an old saying," he told them. "Something like this: *I cried because I had no shoes, and then I met a man who had no feet.*"

"What's that got to do with not being able to have candy bars?" Coby asked crossly.

To Amy's confusion, Ed was watching her with a slight smile. "Amy knows," he said in a gentle tone that encouraged her to speak out.

She swallowed hard. "I guess it means things could be worse, that even if we can't have chocolate, there are other things we can eat, as long as we stay alive."

Ed's smile broadened, and he went on with the things he was taking out of a box to spread out on the table. They had an ominous look to them: peculiar small devices, including what was unquestionably a hypodermic needle.

Amy's stomach muscles contracted so that it was almost like having a cramp. Now, she thought, comes the really tough part. Shots.

"Everybody back? Okay, let's get started, so I can turn you loose before everyone has to go to the bathroom again," Ed said. It seemed strange to Amy to be in a mixed group where people talked openly about having to go to the bathroom. She thought it was making Elizabeth uncomfortable as well, and Joan appeared to be simply furious about everything.

Ed must have noticed that, too. He sat back in his chair, for the moment ignoring those scary-looking objects on the table. "Before we go any further, let's give everybody a chance to say how they feel about having diabetes," he said.

They all stared at him. How could they feel, Amy wondered, except scared and upset?

"Pissed," Coby said. "Madder than hell. Why me?"

There was a small shock wave among the girls. Amy waited, heart beating audibly, for Ed to object to the language. She ought to have known by this time, though, that Ed wasn't strongly judgmental. He simply nodded.

"How about you, Zack? How does it make you feel?"

The red-headed boy was sober. "Scared," he said.

Ed moved on to the youngest member of the group. "Ben?"

The little boy echoed Zack's word in a voice so low they could barely hear it. "Scared. Worried."

"Amy?"

"The same, I guess. Scared and mad, both. I don't know why it happened to me. I didn't do anything to deserve it."

She had never seen a man with such a tender smile. "None of us did, Amy. None of us deserve it, so we don't have to feel guilty about it, do we? There's nothing any of us did to cause us to have diabetes. Some of your parents are feeling guilty, you know, thinking that they passed this along in your genes, but it isn't their fault, either. It's no-body's fault. It just happens to some of us. How do you feel, Elizabeth?"

The very thin girl twisted her hands in her lap. "Like I wish I could just go to sleep and not wake up until it's all over. Like it's a nightmare."

Ed nodded as if he found this reasonable. "Joan?"

Joan had to unclench her jaw to speak. "I hate it. I hate this hospital, and this group, and everything about having diabetes. I want to go home."

Again Ed nodded. "We all want to go home, don't we, kids? We want to go home and be normal again. And it's normal to feel scared and resentful about what's happening to us. Well, we'll go home, and we can be close to normal, if we learn a few things first and follow a few rules."

Coby's tone was low and savage. "No sugar. Lots of exercise. Eat the right things at regular times. Take your insulin when you're supposed to. Check your blood sugar five or six times a day. Oh, it's normal, all right! Just like everybody else."

"I felt angry, too, when I found out," Ed told them. "I'd been a good kid, minded my folks—most of the time—though I'll admit I'd been overeating for years, which was a form of abusing my body. I did well in school, never talked back to teachers, that kind of thing. When I grew up, I got better in school, got my degree in nursing, worked hard at a job. I didn't deserve to get diabetes. Yet I got it, and there was nothing I could do to make it go away. So I learned to live with it, and that's what you're all going to do, too."

He reached forward and picked up the hypodermic needle, and Amy flinched. Beside her, she felt Ben drawing up into a smaller space, too.

"The way we're going to do it is much as Coby says. We're going to change the way we eat, which means cutting back on sugars and fats. Yes, fats, too. That means less fats like butter, using polyunsaturated fats instead most of the time. It doesn't mean you can't have most of the things you like to eat, just that you'll be eating less of some of them and paying more attention to getting a balanced diet. If you don't already eat plenty of raw vegetables and fresh fruit, you'll try to do it from now on. It's a good idea to eat whole grain breads and cereals. You can still eat meats, but you'll try to have more fish and poultry than red meats. Before you leave, each of you will have a session with the dietician so you'll learn about the way to eat that will help you the most, and she'll talk to your moms, too, so they'll know how to cook for you."

Coby made one of his rude noises. "So whose mom cooks?"

"If your mom doesn't do it, you'll have to do it for yourself," Ed said, "because you're the one with diabetes. You're the one who's going to suffer if you don't follow the rules."

"Like what?" Amy blurted, because she couldn't stand it any longer, not knowing. "What'll happen if we don't?"

80

"Well, if you let your blood sugars go too high, you'll feel pretty crummy. You may have severe headaches, you may get sick to your stomach, the way most of you did before you landed in the Emergency Room. You'll feel so tired you can hardly make yourself do anything. Those are the short-term effects of not taking care of yourself. Then there are long-range hazards."

Ed met Amy's eyes as he told her the worst. "If your blood glucose levels stay too high for too long, there may be permanent damage done to your body that can be very serious. Uncontrolled diabetes can cause blindness, and damage to your kidneys and other organs that will make you very sick. It can cause poor circulation, which means that the blood doesn't move as well in your legs and feet as it should; that in turn means that if you injure your foot, for instance, that injury may not heal. We don't talk about those things much because they are less likely to happen if you take care of yourself."

Amy's mouth was dry and she was frightened, but she made herself ask the next question. "What do we have to do, then? Besides eat the right things?"

"You're all going to learn to give yourself insulin. Each one of you is different, so each of your doctors will work out the plan that's best for you. They'll decide which type of insulin you'll take. There are several different types, some of them long-acting, some of them short-acting, and you may take both kinds, or only one kind. You may get by on one shot a day, or you may need two or three."

Amy lost a few of the words Ed was saying, she was so mesmerized by that needle he'd picked up. She couldn't stick one of those into herself, she just couldn't!

Joan made a harsh, rasping sound, and when Amy looked, she saw her own doubts mirrored in Joan's face. Joan, too, was upset and rebellious.

Ed acted as if what he was saying was perfectly ordinary. "We want you to learn how to give your own insulin shots before you leave the hospital. This is a small needle, and it really doesn't hurt very much. I'll show you how to measure out your exact dosage, which is very important. For you younger kids, like Ben and Zack, your parents will probably check that part for a while."

Amy sat silently as Ed went on, explaining just how it worked. He even used the needle on himself, and though he didn't flinch, she thought everyone else did, except Coby and Ginny.

"The first time, we'll let each of you inject an orange," he said. "And some of your dads or moms may let you practice on them before you give your own shots."

Amy stared at the needle he held, knowing that she couldn't stick it in her father or mother any more easily than she could stick it in herself. She felt a wave of hopelessness. How was she ever going to cope with being a diabetic?

By the time the session was over, however, she'd learned what she would have to do. She had seen how to measure out the insulin from the small vials, how to wipe off her skin with alcohol to prevent infection. She'd learned that you had to keep changing the spot where you gave the injection, and that you used your thighs and your stomach and your bottom as well as your upper arms.

She'd seen the strips that were used to do a urine test when a blood test showed that blood glucose was too high, to look for ketones. Ed explained what Ginny had said earlier about being in ketosis, or ketoacidosis.

"I know this is a lot of new words for you to handle all at once, but some of them are important. Like ketones, or acetone. This is an acid that builds up when you have too little insulin, and your body starts burning stored fat for energy because that's all it can get at without the insulin. If you get very much of this acid, when your blood sugar is building up, it makes you pretty sick. Most of you were feeling that way when you came to the hospital; if you had been left untreated, you would have been even sicker. So if your ketones build up—when that happens you may have a distinctive odor on your breath, which is one clue to help us diagnose diabetes—

you need to take immediate action. This can happen when you have too little insulin in your bloodstream; you may go into diabetic coma, which is dangerous.''

He explained that too much insulin could cause an insulin reaction in which a diabetic could become unconscious and even die.

''The important thing is to keep your food and your exercise and your insulin in balance. If possible, you should eat at the same time every day, and not go long periods between meals. You'll probably need snacks at mid-morning, in the afternoon, and at bedtime, to maintain the right balance. And you'll want to carry sugar cubes or hard candies like Life Savers to eat quickly if your blood sugar drops too low; you'll learn, by the way you feel, when that's happening, though that doesn't mean you can skip blood testing to be sure just because you feel okay. You can also have orange juice if it's available, which will quickly correct the balance so you'll feel better. It sounds more complicated than it is, because you'll soon learn by how different things make you feel.''

He told them that exercising, or not exercising, could cause a change in blood glucose levels, and that it was a good idea to eat an apple or maybe a sandwich before exercise, and to stop and eat something with sugar in it at once if they felt peculiar.

''There will be times when your blood sugar levels

will vary because of stress—when you're upset or angry about something—or when you're sick. You must *always* take your insulin, even when you're ill. If you're not sure how much to take, because you aren't able to eat as much as usual, call your doctor or someone on the staff here at the hospital to be sure. Remember this: if your diabetes is under good control, you'll probably feel good. But you can't take it for granted that if you don't feel sick, you're doing okay. You have to check, *every day*, to be sure. And this is how you check."

Ed went on to the other devices he had in his collection on the table. There were several of them that held little disposable needles with which to prick one's finger to get a drop of blood. The blood was put on a slim plastic strip, left for one minute, then wiped off; you counted another minute and then compared the colors at the end of the strip with those on the container it had come in, to read the level of your blood sugar.

An uneasy murmur ran around the room when Ed said he was going to test everyone right then. Amy felt as if her stomach flopped over, and she actually jerked when he said, "Let's start with Amy. Which finger do you think has blood in it, Amy?"

As a joke, it wasn't much. Ed loaded the device, which was like a thick pen, and handed it to her. "Stick the side of any finger, here on the first joint, see? Hold it like this, and then just flip that little lever. It's easier to let the finger sticker do it than to stab it in yourself."

It took all her courage to use her thumb to release the little needle. It stung, though only for a moment, and then the drop of blood grew and dripped onto the reagent strip while Amy counted off sixty seconds on the watch Ed had put before her. "When you're doing this at home," Ed said while they waited, "you don't have to clean your finger with alcohol first. Just wash your hands with soap and water. Ginny can tell you why that's important, can't you, Ginny?"

The minute was up, and nervously Amy wiped away the blood. The little squares on the end of the plastic strip stared up at her accusingly, though she hadn't eaten anything but what the hospital staff had given her, and she'd had insulin that morning.

"Sure," Ginny said. "One day I got in a panic because when I checked my blood sugar it was 400, and I'm supposed to keep it about 120. I didn't feel sick, but it scared me, and Mom rushed me over to the doctor's office. I felt really stupid when we figured out what had happened. I'd eaten sweet pickles, and some of the juice was still on my fingers when I did the blood test. I forgot to wash my hands. So it contaminated the blood specimen."

"Don't forget, though," Ed reminded, "that if something appears to be wrong, consult with the doctor. Don't worry about looking foolish if you've simply made a mistake. We'd rather have you feel foolish than get into real trouble. Time's up, Amy. What did you get?"

Amy picked up the plastic strip and held it alongside the colored squares on the container. "One hundred and twenty?" she asked uncertainly, matching the colors.

"Sure looks like it. Right where it ought to be. Who's next? Joan?"

Amy gave an inward sigh of relief. She still didn't think she was ever going to get used to this, but she was over the first hurdle. She was glad now Ed had made her go first, so she didn't have to keep on worrying about doing the blood test. She could relax and watch everybody else. She'd worry about the insulin injection when the time came.

Joan was biting her lip and looking at the finger sticker as if it were a venomous snake.

Amy heard her own voice, much to her surprise, saying, "It's really not that bad, Joan. It only stings for a few seconds."

It was true, she realized. She didn't look forward to doing it every day, several times a day, but she'd survived, hadn't she?

Across the table she caught Coby's eyes upon her. He winked.

Confused and embarrassed, Amy shifted her own gaze away from him. To Joan, who lifted the finger sticker with a trembling hand and swallowed hard before she flipped the lever that sent the needle stabbing into her finger.

Amazingly, Amy was more aware of Coby, watching her, than she was of Joan and her blood testing. She didn't know why the boy was looking at her, but it made her feel sort of excited as well as embarrassed. She wondered if Danny Crowell would ever look at her that way, and then was surprised again to realize she was thinking something so normal. For a while, she'd wondered if she'd ever think anything normal again.

10.

Their beds had been made up while they were away from their room. Amy hesitated in the doorway. "Do we have to go back to bed, do you think?"

Ginny shook her head. "No. We can stretch out on top of the bedspreads and leave on our regular clothes, as long as we feel okay. I guess I'm going home tomorrow; my blood sugar seems to be all right. Do you feel better, too?"

Amy climbed onto the edge of the high bed; her feet dangled off the floor. She thought about the candy bar under her pillow at home and wondered who'd get to eat it. "Some. I'm awfully mixed-up,

89

though. I don't remember half of what Ed said today, all the complicated stuff."

"Don't worry. You won't kill yourself by making a mistake," Ginny assured her. "When you start to feel rotten, then you know you have to do something about it. Most of the time you're counting on the insulin to keep your blood sugar from getting too high, but if you get too much insulin, or go too long without eating anything, the blood sugar drops too low. You get crabby and tired and shaky, maybe nervous and sweaty, or sometimes real hungry. Then you eat some of the sugar they won't let you have the rest of the time, and within five or ten minutes you'll be okay. Diabetes is crazy."

"It sure is," Amy said with feeling. "Do you really get used to it? So you don't mind it?"

Ginny made a face. "Well, I wouldn't go so far as to say I don't *mind* it. It's a pain to have to remember to eat something before P.E. class so you don't get dizzy and pass out. That happened to me once when I'd left my Life Savers in my locker instead of taking them to class with me. And once I had this teacher—she was a substitute and didn't know anything about diabetes—refuse to let me leave the class to get my crackers and cheese from my locker. Most of my teachers are swell."

Amy drew up her feet and sat cross-legged, Indian fashion. "What kinds of things does diabetes keep you from doing?" She could still write stories, she thought. And Pudge could keep on doing the illustrations for them. If Pudge kept on being her friend now that Amy had diabetes, that was. There was nothing Pudge loved better than going to the Dairy Queen for a cheeseburger and a double hot fudge sundae, and there was no way Amy intended to go along and watch her eat that when she couldn't have a sundae herself.

"It doesn't keep me from doing anything," Ginny said.

Amy blinked. "Really? Nothing at all?"

"Well, I miss being able to pig out on ice cream with chocolate syrup on it, the way I used to. Now I just have plain ice cream, and only a small serving. And I can't have seconds on spaghetti or refried beans because they make my sugar go up, though not everybody has trouble with those, and of course I drink diet pop and eat diet Jell-O instead of ice cream bars. But I can go to the drive-in with the other kids when they eat; there's always something I can have. I play soccer and swim, and when school starts I'm going to start gymnastics lessons twice a week. My sister's had lessons for over a year, and she's taught me a little bit."

Amy hesitated, then asked before she lost her nerve, "Did you ever wet the bed?"

"Sure. Before we knew I was diabetic, I mean. I was at my grandma's house, and she was kind of upset, wanted to know why I didn't get up and go to the bathroom. After she found out it was because of the diabetes, she felt bad she'd been cross about it. She took me to Seattle and bought me three new outfits for school."

"But you don't wet the bed any more?"

"Not since that one time, no. My mom knew there must be something the matter when she heard about that time, and then I got really sick and landed in here. It was a relief to know it wasn't my fault."

Amy nodded. "To me, too. I didn't dare go stay with my best friend for fear I'd wet the bed over there. Do you stay overnight away from home now?"

"Sure, when I want to. It makes me feel kind of funny the first time I do it at a new place, if they don't know about my diabetes. Once I went to stay for the weekend with Tammy, and her mom found my insulin and stuff—you know, the needles and all—and she nearly had a fit, thinking I was a drug addict. I thought she was going to call the cops before Tammy could explain. It was embarrassing."

"I guess," Amy agreed, imagining it. Except that Pudge's mother knew about the diabetes, and would want to hear all the details about the blood testing and shots and everything. She'd never call the police about anything Amy did.

Ginny suddenly shot her a sideways look from under her lashes. "You like Coby?"

"What?" Amy said. She'd heard, but she was startled and didn't know what to reply to the question.

"Coby. You like him? I noticed he was watching you while we were down in the Peds lounge. And he threw you the pancreas pillow."

Amy's cheeks got warm. "I don't even know him. He's kind of mouthy."

"Yeah. My mom thinks it's because he's defensive. He likes to use words that shock people sometimes. Though in here everybody uses plain words. Lots of the kids don't know the right words for things. If you talked about urination they wouldn't know what you meant. That's why Ed doesn't stop him from talking plain or even cussing once in a while. Ed likes Coby a lot; he hates to see him come in here because he gets sick."

"Why does he? I mean, is Coby sick because he doesn't follow the rules? Because he does the wrong things? On purpose?" The idea made her uneasy. Just how bad would the problems get if she broke the rules?

Ginny was nodding her head, swinging her feet back and forth high off the floor. "He breaks the rules, all right. I've seen him smoking, for one thing. I don't think he inhales, and he isn't addicted yet; so far he's just doing it to show off for the older kids. Ed's told him how stupid it is. I mean, smoking is stupid for anybody, don't you think, when it causes cancer and heart disease and all that stuff?

But it's worse for a diabetic. I think Coby drinks sometimes, too, and that's even harder to understand, even if it weren't dangerous for a diabetic."

"Why?" Amy asked. "I mean, why does he do it, then? He seemed mouthy, but he didn't seem stupid."

"No, he's not stupid. He's actually a pretty good student, when he comes to school. He gets in trouble and misses a lot, but he works to make it up so he can be on the teams. He plays just about every sport, and he's good at all of them.

"I don't know. Maybe it's just showing off again. I should think he wouldn't touch anything with alcohol in it, because his dad's a drunk. He hates it that his dad spends every night drinking beer. Maybe he doesn't really drink very much but wants the kids to think he does. I don't know. Coby's kind of weird."

Amy felt shocked, thinking about Coby's dad being a drunk. She'd hate it, too, if everyone knew something like that about her dad.

Ginny slid off the bed. "Come on, let's go find him. Maybe he feels like talking."

Amy opened her mouth to protest that she wasn't interested in chasing any boy around—especially one like Coby—but Ginny was already going out the door.

On second thought, Amy closed her mouth and followed.

Coby wasn't in his room. In fact he wasn't even on Peds, as Amy had begun to think of their floor because that's what everyone else called it.

"He got on the elevator and went to the fourth floor," a smiling aide told them when Ginny asked. "Visiting, I guess."

It seemed strange to Amy that anyone sick enough to be in the hospital would be allowed to wander around at will. "What's on the fourth floor?" she asked as Ginny punched the button for the elevator.

"Geriatrics. That's old people."

That didn't sound like Coby's choice of patients to visit, Amy thought, and saw Ginny grin, reading her mind.

"Coby likes old people. His grandpa died two years ago, and I think he misses him a lot. His grandpa used to take him to Seahawks games, and they talked. I don't think his own dad talks to him much, nor his mother, either. When my grandma was on the fourth floor, we met Coby there, just visiting some of the old people he met when his grandpa was in here the last time."

The elevator doors opened, they got on, and Ginny pushed the button for the fourth floor. Amy wasn't sure why they were following Coby around. If he was talking to someone, he might not appreciate being interrupted. But she followed along after Ginny anyway. Anything was better than sitting in her room thinking about being diabetic for the rest of her life, dreading having to start giving herself shots.

They found Coby in the lounge playing checkers with a cheerful looking old man in a wheelchair who had his foot in a cast and an IV on a portable stand running some kind of fluid into his arm.

As they approached, Coby moved a checker, and the old man gave a cackle of delight. "Gotcha!" he cried, and jumped his own man, making Coby laugh and lean back in his chair.

"Okay, you won again. I'm gonna quit playing you if you keep winning," Coby said. "Hi, Ginny. Hi, Amy. You know Mr. Gambini? He runs the Mini-Mart on Grove Street."

The girls greeted Mr. Gambini, who was pleased about winning the game. Amy remembered him now; she'd been in the market a few times with Matt when they'd gone fishing early in the morning and wanted to pick up some extra snacks to take along.

"Sit down, sit down," the old man urged. "This boy is the only young face I've seen in this place."

"What happened to you?" Ginny wanted to know.

"Got hit by a truck," Mr. Gambini said. "Well, a pickup truck, anyway. Feller ran a red light, and I wasn't watching close enough. Lucky I didn't get killed."

Amy thought of her own narrow escape and shivered.

Coby folded up the checkerboard and put the

checkers into a box. "You don't belong on fourth floor. You're not old enough."

That seemed to tickle Mr. Gambini. "You're right, boy. I don't belong up here. I belong down wherever they're keeping the young people, not with a bunch of old fogies."

"Are you going to have to be here a long time?" Ginny asked, looking at the cast.

"Oh, no. No more'n a few days, I guess. Then I'll have to learn to walk with a crutch, they tell me."

"It's easy," Coby said, scratching his chest so that the diabetes I.D. tag got pushed to one side. "I broke my ankle sliding into third base last summer, and I was on crutches for the rest of the season. It's the only reason my team didn't win first place; they didn't have me to hit for 'em."

Mr. Gambini laughed. "I'll bet you're telling the truth, except that when you're seventy-three it's not so easy to learn new tricks, like using crutches. Don't know quite how I'm going to keep the Mini-Mart going, hobbling around on one leg. Got to hang onto the crutches, don't you? Make it hard to put up my stock. How long you going to be in here, boy?"

Coby flipped his head so his hair lifted off his forehead, then settled back into the same position. "I'm leaving tomorrow. I got a ball game to win."

Mr. Gambini winked at the girls. "Thinks well of himself, don't he? Well, I been thinking, too.

Until I get rid of this confounded cast and those crutches I haven't even learned to use yet, I could do with some help at the Mini-Mart. How about you coming over to do the heavy stuff for me? My wife's keeping the place open, but she can't lift much. Pay you minimum wage. You got a Social Security card?"

"Sure," Coby said readily. "I mean, I got a card. And I'll take the job."

Mr. Gambini winked again. "Maybe he'll spend all I pay him on candy bars and pop, so I'll get it all back," he said.

Amy tensed up, but Ginny didn't. "He better not, unless he wants to wind up in here again," she said. "Coby's diabetic, just like we are."

The old man's smile faded. "That right? Can't have any candy, eh?"

"I do if I want," Coby said.

"And you get sick," Ginny pointed out. "What's the point? My brother said you're a really good ball-player. You'll probably make the high school team this year. Maybe even win a scholarship to college. Why blow it by eating stuff you aren't supposed to have?"

Coby gave her a cool look, but Amy thought there was a flicker of interest in his eyes. "Your brother said that? The brother that's on the football team?"

"Yes, Jimmy. There're plenty of sweet things you

can still eat, the way the rest of us do. Diet pop's not bad, fruit's okay."

"Diabetic candy's not so great," Coby challenged.

"My mom just got a cookbook, *The Diabetic Chocolate Cookbook*," Ginny said. "I'm going to try making some candy for Christmas. I won't be able to have much of it at one time, but the recipes sound good." She turned to Amy. "You want to come over and try some of them with me?"

"Sure," Amy heard herself saying, and then felt peculiar. Would it hurt Pudge's feelings if Amy made a new friend of Ginny?

"If it comes out good, bring me some," Coby suggested.

"Me, too," Mr. Gambini said. "I'm not diabetic, but I weigh too much. Besides, I want to see how smart the young people are these days."

Coby looked at the clock. "Smart enough to know it's nearly suppertime. We better go back to Peds so we can have our well-balanced meal, right? See you tomorrow, Mr. Gambini, before I leave."

"Right. And you'll come work for me, eh?"

Ginny spoke softly as the girls headed for the elevator ahead of Coby. "Be good for him to be around Mr. Gambini. Maybe he'll get some sense and quit doing things that land him in here. Come on, let's find out what the terrific diabetic dessert is going to be tonight, okay?"

The dessert turned out to be low calorie Jell-O with low calorie whipped cream, and to be truthful Amy couldn't tell the difference from the regular kind.

She wasn't thinking about the dessert, though. She was thinking about the session tomorrow, when she'd have to give herself that first shot.

11.

Pudge came again that evening and brought Natalie. They stopped uncertainly in the doorway when they saw that Amy had a roommate and that both of them were sitting up, fully dressed, reading.

Natalie was carrying a bouquet of daisies and red and yellow roses, the stems wrapped in damp paper towels. Pudge had a package wrapped in colorful paper with ladybugs all over it.

Amy put down her book. "Come on in." She introduced them to Ginny, who also put aside her book and slid off the bed. "Pretty flowers. Want me to get a vase for them?"

Without waiting for a reply, Ginny left the room,

leaving the visitors looking after her in bewilderment.

"Is she a patient?" Pudge asked.

"Yes. She's diabetic, too." Amy got off the bed. "Is the package for me, too?"

Pudge handed it over, then couldn't wait for Amy to open it. "It's a hardcover book with blank pages, for you to do your next story. You can leave every other page blank, and I'll do the illustrations for it, and then you'll have a real book, to keep. I couldn't decide if you'd rather have red or blue, so I got red. Okay?"

Amy admired the book. "I'll have to write something really special for this one."

Natalie handed over the flowers when Ginny returned with a vase. "All I've been hearing about is your stories. I hope you'll let me read some of them when you get home."

Ed Soldenski stuck his head into the room. "I'm going off duty, girls. I guess you'll be gone before I come on tomorrow, Ginny, so good-bye and be good, and I won't see you again soon. I'll meet you in the lounge at ten, Amy."

He didn't specify what for, but Amy knew. Her stomach tightened in apprehension.

Pudge and Natalie were staring at the empty space where the nurse had been.

"Who was that?" Pudge breathed in awe.

"Ed. The nurse who teaches kids about diabetes."

102

"Wow," Natalie said softly. "I never had a nurse like that when *I* was in the hospital."

"What were you in for?" Pudge wanted to know.

Natalie hesitated, glanced at Ginny, who was back to reading her book, and spoke softly. "I feel stupid, admitting it."

"What'd you do? Get a drug overdose?" Pudge asked.

"No, stupid." Then Natalie blushed. "I guess it was just about that dumb. I had bulimia."

Amy and Pudge looked at each other. Neither of them knew what she was talking about.

Ginny did, though. She rested her book on her stomach. "Where you eat all the time, and then make yourself throw up?"

"On purpose?" Pudge asked, horrified.

"Yes. It sounds horrible—it *was* horrible, actually—and my folks put me in the hospital because I couldn't quit. I even wondered"—she hesitated, glancing at Amy—"if you had bulimia, too, when I saw how much you were eating at the Dairy Queen. Only I couldn't quite ask. I never told anybody about me before," Natalie confessed. "Some things you don't want anybody to know, but I guess none of you will spread it around."

"I know what you mean," Amy said, but she wasn't quite ready, yet, to confess to wetting the bed, even though she now knew it was the diabetes that had caused it, not her own carelessness.

"If you guys want to sit and talk," Ginny suggested, "why don't you go down to the lounge? If there's nobody else there, you can have some privacy. The chairs in here aren't very comfortable even if there were enough of them to go around."

"It's strange, you being able to walk wherever you want," Pudge said as they went along the hallway. "I thought if you were in the hospital you had to stay in bed. Are you going to get to come home tomorrow?"

"I don't know yet. Nobody's mentioned it," Amy said, feeling that uncomfortable sensation again in the pit of her stomach. "Maybe it depends on how fast I can learn to give myself shots."

The lounge was empty, and they sat and talked for a while. Clearly Pudge was spending time with Natalie, and Amy was sort of mixed-up in her feelings about it. Natalie *did* seem nice, and she'd shared a secret with Amy as well as with Pudge. And now Ginny had invited Amy to come over and learn how to make diabetic candy so she could have sweets at least as a rare treat. That seemed better than never tasting chocolate again for the rest of her life.

"I guess we better go," Pudge said after a while. "I think that's your brother and your folks talking to the nurse, Amy. They'll want to visit. Let me know when you get to come home, okay?"

"Okay. And thanks for the book, and the flowers." Amy stood up with them, then found the way to the elevator blocked by a now familiar figure in blue jeans and a blue shirt.

"Hey, Amy. There you are. I just wanted to say good-bye, and good luck."

She felt paralyzed, tongue-tied. Coby had actually sought her out to speak to her before he left. She made her mouth work. "Are you leaving tonight?"

"Yeah. Old vampire Soldenski told my doctor I was as rehabilitated as he could manage for this session." He grinned, and again she saw that he could be quite attractive, not at all the way he was when he was sullen and mouthing off. "See you around," he said, lifting a hand, and was gone toward the elevators.

"Gee," Natalie observed, "you've met some interesting people in here, Amy."

"That's Coby Bonner. He's diabetic, too," Amy said. She felt both embarrassed and pleased that Coby had made a point of telling her good-bye.

Pudge sighed. "Boys never talk to me. Do you think it's because I'm too fat?"

"You're not fat," Amy said quickly.

"Just a little plump," Natalie added. She didn't seem to notice that she'd wounded Pudge. Maybe Natalie wasn't as perfect as she could be, Amy thought. Not tactful, anyway.

She walked to meet her parents and Matt after her friends had gone, wondering if Dr. Rosenbaum had left orders that she could go home tomorrow;

105

she did want to go home, but she was still afraid of what she'd have to manage to do by herself once she got there.

She had trouble going to sleep that night, and she woke up remembering immediately that she was meeting Ed and the other kids at ten, to learn about the shots. Just before the meeting, Ginnie went home. Amy was surprised at how upset she was to see her go. Ginnie really was a friend.

In the Peds lounge, nobody else looked any happier than Amy felt. Joan stopped biting her fingernails when Amy came in, but didn't say anything. The room seemed different without Coby and Ginnie.

"Hi," Ed said easily, looking up from the paraphernalia spread out on the table. "Everybody get comfortable, and we'll get started. I want each of you to do a finger stick all by yourself, just to make sure you understand how to do it. Joan's mother is going to get one of the machines that gives you a digital reading of your blood sugar; the rest of you will be using the glucose strips like those we had yesterday. The machine is more exact, though in most cases we don't have to be that particular, and it's more expensive, so many people just do it this way."

They all took seats, and nobody else seemed any

more at ease than Amy was. Joan was biting her fingernails again. Elizabeth kept pleating and repleating the fabric of her skirt between her fingers, and Ben and Zack just looked scared.

"Until just a few years ago," Ed told them, "the only way to measure blood sugar levels was with a urine test. It was better than nothing, but there were some problems with it. The difficulty is that when the sugar starts to build up in your blood it has to get quite high before it spills over into your urine and can be detected there. You can get pretty sick before you realize what's going on, because testing your urine tells you what your blood sugar was several hours earlier, not what it is at the present. Though you know what the glucose in your urine is, the level in your blood may have changed considerably. So if you think you have a lot of sugar, and take extra insulin to make up for it, you may get too much insulin because the glucose level has already dropped."

He looked at Zack. "What happens then, if you get too much insulin?"

Zack moistened his lips. "You get sick."

"And what do you do about that?"

The boy hesitated, and Ed looked at Elizabeth. "You remember?"

"You take something with sugar in it. Orange juice, or hard candy like Life Savers."

"Right. You're going to carry those with you all the time, don't forget. Now there is one time when you'll do urine testing, and I'll show you how to do that, too. It's when you think you may be in ketoacidosis, so you'll check for ketones in your urine. Right now, though, we'll go with the blood testing. Ready?"

Ed opened the vial and took out some of the plastic strips, passing them around. "Everybody just wash their hands? Good. Handle these carefully, now. Don't touch the end with the colored squares; you want to get an accurate reading of what's in your blood, not what's left on your finger. The exciting thing about blood testing is that it tells you what your sugar level is right now, this minute, not what it was several hours ago, the way the urine test does. So you know immediately whether you need to eat, need more insulin, or are okay until it's time to test again. Who can tell me what affects your blood sugar levels? Amy?"

"What you eat," Amy said. "If you eat too much, or the wrong things, it goes up. If you don't eat enough, it goes too low and you have . . ." She hesitated, because she'd never said the word before, and wasn't sure she could pronounce it correctly. ". . . have hypo—hypoglycemia."

Ed nodded, smiling. "Good. You're learning the words, and you're learning the concepts. Now, one

108

at a time since we only have one watch to time this by, each of you is going to do your blood test. And then we'll see how easy it is to give yourself an insulin injection. Joan, you want to start?"

It was clear that Joan didn't want anything to do with the process. Amy sat huddled in her own anxieties as first Joan, and then Elizabeth, pricked their fingers and did the tests. Then it was Amy's turn. She loaded the device with the needle, held it against the side of her finger. She held her breath and closed her eyes before she flipped the lever.

It stung momentarily, and then the drop of blood appeared. She held it over the glucose strip covered the reagent pads, and looked at the watch. Sixty seconds, wipe it off, then another sixty seconds and compare it with the colors on the container.

One hundred and twenty. Right where it ought to be. She gave an inaudible sigh of relief. She was sweating, though the room wasn't warm. Eventually, she supposed, she'd get used to doing this.

Ed stuck needles into himself without flinching or changing expression from his usual smile. "Okay, now watch and I'll show you how to draw the right quantity of insulin out of the bottle. Remember, alcohol to clean everything. We'll do this one in the orange, Elizabeth. You get to start. I'll demonstrate, and then you do it."

Elizabeth swallowed visibly, steeling herself even

to touch the needle. She was very pale, but she watched Ed, and then did the same thing he had done.

"Good! If you can do it in the orange, you can do it in yourself."

If Coby were there, he'd say, "Sure, but the orange doesn't hurt," Amy thought. Her mouth was dry, and she had a cramp as if she'd been running hard. And then it was her turn; she drew up the insulin, depressed the plunger on the needle with shaking fingers, then passed the orange along to Joan.

When it was time to try the procedure on themselves, Ed suggested starting with an easy place to reach. "Your stomach is right there in front of you. Let's try there. Grab hold of your belly like this, make it stick up in a hump, and put the needle straight in. Remember, it's a tiny needle, and it's coated so it will go in easily. It won't sting even as much as the finger stick did, okay?"

Joan refused. "I can't," she said. "I can't do it."

Amy thought he'd insist, but he didn't. Instead he turned to her. "Ready, Amy?"

She supposed she was as ready as she'd ever be. Her fingers were icy, yet slippery with sweat. The hypodermic needle felt awkward, and she had to take a deep breath and use all her courage.

And then it was over, to her relief and surprise; she'd done it. She'd injected her own insulin.

110

Ed was grinning at her. "Excellent!"

For the first time in quite a while Amy felt good about herself, and she grinned back, even if the grin was a little shaky.

12.

$\mathbf{E}$lizabeth, too, was triumphant and tremulous. She grinned at Amy as they left the lounge. "I never thought I could do it."

"I wasn't sure, either," Amy confessed. "Ginny said you get used to it. I expect it'll be a long time before I can just pick up that needle and push the plunger into my own stomach without shaking, though. I'm glad the first time is over with."

"Me, too. I have to practice some more, because I guess I'm going home today, when my mom and dad get here," Elizabeth said. She glanced over her shoulder, to where only Joan remained in the Peds lounge with Ed Soldenski. "I don't know if she's going to learn to give her own shots or not."

"They won't let her go home until she does, will they?" Amy wondered.

They walked back to their rooms. Elizabeth waved a hand. "Good luck," she said.

"Yeah, you too," Amy replied. It seemed strange when she entered the hospital room not to find Ginny there. Of course, she'd be going home herself soon.

She had mixed feelings about it. On one hand, she was eager to be away from this place, to go home to family and friends. Yet she felt changed now, different. How would other people look at her, knowing she had diabetes? She knew it wasn't catching, but there might be kids who wouldn't be sure of that.

And when school started, in just a couple of weeks, everybody would know. Ed had already given her several pamphlets to pass along to her teachers and the principal, so they'd know what to do in an emergency.

"Educate everybody around you about reactions when you get too much insulin because you don't eat enough, or have too much exercise without eating. Remember, you have to keep your food, exercise, and insulin in the proper balance at all times. If you feel hungry, sweaty, shaky, nervous, or weak, you'll need to eat something at once, so make sure everyone around you knows that so they can help if you need it."

It was an unsettling thought, that people around her would have to be aware of her diabetes. She would rather have kept it a secret, like wetting the bed. She didn't want people to think she was different, yet it seemed necessary that they should.

"Most diabetics wear either an I.D. bracelet or one of these." Ed had flipped the disc he wore on a chain around his neck. "That's so if something happens and you can't speak out yourself, and you need medical treatment, people will know you're diabetic. Adult diabetics have sometimes been mistakenly considered drunk when they were having a reaction, and thrown into jail instead of taken to a hospital for emergency medical treatment."

Amy put the coupon to send for the diabetic I.D. bracelet into her suitcase with the rest of the things she was going to take home. It would be just like branding her forehead, she thought, telling everyone she had diabetes. That she was different. Yet even Coby wore the I.D.

"You aren't as different as you think," Ed had told the group. It was almost as if he could read their minds. "There are an estimated twelve million diabetics in this country, with six hundred thousand more being diagnosed every year. So you've got lots of company. If everybody followed the diabetic diet, which is just good nutritious food with the proper proportions of fats, proteins, and carbohydrates, many of the people who will now get diabetes might not get it, or at least not for many years."

Amy wished she hadn't gotten diabetes. Sometimes she pretended she hadn't, that it was only a bad dream, that she would go home and forget about it. But she couldn't pretend for very long at a time.

"There's another thing you and your parents should be aware of," Ed had said, and they'd known he was serious. "And that is that a diabetic has to take most of the responsibility for his or her own care. Not only do you have to be the one to decide what you'll eat, and how much healthy exercise you'll get, and pay attention to taking your insulin on time, but in an emergency you had better know what to do."

He had leaned toward them, his eyes intent. "Unfortunately there is so much to know in the medical profession that no one doctor can possibly know everything about everything. And there are some doctors who don't know very much about diabetes. There are still quite a few of them who haven't learned how much more accurate a blood test is than a urine test, because they don't have time to read all the new information that's being published about caring for diabetics."

He twisted the I.D. chain between his fingers. "You could go to a hospital Emergency Room needing immediate help, and if there is no diabetes education program there like the one we have here, the nurses or doctors on duty might not know exactly what they should do to help you right away. That's why you need to know, and your parents need to know. One very important thing I try to convey to the parents of diabetic kids is that it's okay to be aggressive on behalf of their child in an emergency. If the parent knows what to do—and all of yours do, I've talked to them the same as I've talked to you kids—he or she can insist on the proper procedures to help you in an emergency."

"What about a P.E. teacher who won't let you go get your snack when you start feeling woozy from exercise?" Amy had asked, remembering Ginnie's experience.

Ed had nodded. "Sometimes you'll have to speak out forcefully on your own behalf, when you know you're right. You're the diabetic, you know about your own condition and what's best for you to do. Mostly people will respect that when you explain."

All of that kept going through Amy's head. She had learned a lot, but she had to practice giving the shots some more before she'd be very confident about it. She was still scared. She was afraid she'd make mistakes, and she dreaded having everybody at school know about her condition.

"Amy?"

She turned to see Elizabeth in the doorway, carrying a small overnight bag.

116

"I'm leaving in a minute. My mom's still talking to the doctor, and I wanted to tell you what I overheard."

Amy walked toward her. "What?" she asked.

"Joan has the same doctor I have. Her mother was talking to him and Ed, and I overheard part of it."

"Aren't they going to let her go home if she won't give herself the shots?"

"Oh, she's going home. Her mother says she'll give her the shots. I asked my mom about that, but she said I'd better learn to do it myself, though she'll help inject the awkward places. Anyway, Ed and Dr. Adams tried to tell Joan's mother that it was better for a kid to learn all this stuff herself, that kids who are in control handle everything better than ones who get babied. Ben gave himself a shot, and he's only seven. They can't make Joan do it herself, though, if her folks don't cooperate. I just thought you'd like to know." Elizabeth smiled. "Maybe someday they'll come up with a cure for diabetes, a real one they can use on all of us. I know Ed said they've done some pancreas transplants that've been successful, and they've transplanted those islets that make insulin into a diabetic, and they grew and worked. Maybe we'll meet back here for surgery, or they'll discover something else that'll make us normal again, so we don't have to give ourselves shots the rest of our lives."

"We'll probably still have to do finger sticks," Amy said, but she was smiling too. "Unless they find out that transplanting the islets works on everybody. Or they develop a way to take insulin in pills, instead of in shots. Be great, wouldn't it? Good luck, Elizabeth."

"Yeah. Good luck," Elizabeth echoed, and then she was gone.

Amy put the rest of her things in her bag and sat down to wait for her mother to come. They were to have one more session with the dietician before she went home. At least she wasn't scared of that—she wouldn't have to stick herself with needles.

She didn't know how she felt about Joan, except sorry for her. For herself, Amy was glad she'd done the injection, that she knew how and wasn't quite so frightened of it as she had been.

Amy knew there was a lot of research going on about diabetes. She hoped they *would* come up with a cure, and soon. The transplanting of the cells that made insulin was still in an experimental stage, and she wasn't sure how she felt about having surgery for such a thing. Her dad said it would probably be years before the procedure was perfected, so not to hold her breath waiting for it.

For now, she had to learn to cope with things the way they were. She was glad when her mother appeared in the doorway and said, smiling, "Come on, Amy, let's go see the dietician, and then we'll go home."

"Good," Amy said, smiling back.

They'd talked to the dietician, Mrs. Rose, before. She had asked what time Amy got up, and when she ate each of her meals, and helped work out a schedule she would follow from now on. She would have to eat at regular times, to keep that food/insulin balance. They'd talked about what foods Amy especially liked, and what she wouldn't be able to have now, and which things she could find substitutes for. Mrs. Long had bought a cookbook called *How to Have Your Cake and Eat It, Too!* and it was somewhat reassuring to know that she wouldn't have to give up desserts totally. There was even a section on how to eat out in a restaurant or a drive-in.

Today's session wasn't long; they went over Amy's program, and Mrs. Rose made sure she understood it. When she walked them to the door, the dietician smiled. "Don't forget. I'm here, at the other end of your telephone line, if you have questions. Just give me a call when you have a problem, and we'll work it out."

Amy's heart was thudding as they headed for the elevator. Would she be able to follow all the rules? To avoid mistakes, so she wouldn't have to come back here? And to get along at school when everyone found out she was diabetic?

119

Her mother gave her a hug. "It's going to be okay, Amy. We'll work out the problems, whatever they are."

Amy tried to smile as she hugged back. "I'm scared, Mom."

"I know. It scares me, too, though not as much as it did when Dr. Rosenbaum first told us you had diabetes. We've learned a lot, and we can handle it."

The elevator doors slid open, and they got on. Amy hoped her mother was right, because it was the biggest problem she'd ever had, and she didn't know if she was brave enough, or smart enough, to cope with it.

Her mother was watching her, and maybe she read Amy's doubts on her face. She put her arm around Amy's shoulders and held her close as the elevator descended. "We can do it, Amy."

"Yeah, I guess," Amy agreed.

But it was still only she who had to be on the diet, she thought, and give herself the shots. She drew in a deep breath when they walked off the elevator and out of the hospital into the sunshine. It was a surprise that everything looked so normal when her whole life had been turned so completely around.

On the way home, when her mother reached out to take her hand, Amy squeezed it back, yet she felt a prickle of tears that she could not help.

120

13.

It felt strange to be home again. Jan looked at her as if she were afraid Amy might have grown horns, or wings. "Do you hurt or anything?"

Amy laughed ruefully. "Or anything, I guess. No, I don't hurt, and I don't feel sick. Except maybe for a minute or so before I have to stick myself for the blood test, or give the shot. Dr. Rosenbaum thinks I'm going to have to have two shots a day; Elizabeth has to have three." Zack, she remembered, expected to have to have only one.

"Do the shots hurt a lot?" Jan's blue eyes were big. Amy could just imagine what she was thinking: *I'm glad it's not me who has to have them.* It was a feeling she'd have a lot over the next few days, that people were glad it was her and not them who had diabetes, though of course no one said anything like that.

Gram let go of her walker long enough to hug Amy, then held up the needles with the variegated orange, white, and brown yarn on them. "It's going to be pretty, isn't it? It won't take long, with my having to just sit all the time, to get it finished." She hesitated, then hugged Amy again. "It's good to have you home, child."

Matt was probably the most normal-acting. He punched her on the shoulder and said, "Get your junk out of the way, okay, before somebody breaks their neck on it?" as he kicked at her small suitcase.

Amy stuck her tongue out at him and shoved the suitcase aside. "I'll take it when I go upstairs."

"I'll get it now," Matt decided. "After all, the vampires have been at you. With all that blood loss, you're probably too weak to carry it."

Actually, she wasn't feeling weak. In fact, she felt better than she had in weeks, though she wasn't ready to take up running with Matt yet.

"What vampires?" Jan wanted to know.

"That's what one of the kids called Ed—Mr. Soldenski, the nurse—because he was always taking blood samples for the lab. Vampires suck your blood, you know, like in horror movies."

"Oh." Jan looked as if she thought Amy was going to self-destruct right in front of her.

"Hey, it's me, Amy. I've got diabetes, and I have to take shots and I can't eat stuff with a lot of sugar, but I'm not a freak," Amy said.

"Yeah, I know. Mom told me," Jan said.

In spite of her own words, Amy felt somewhat like a freak. Being diabetic meant a lot of change in her life, much of it related to food.

She didn't need to eat so much she smuggled it into her room anymore. But the fact that everybody else could have things she couldn't have was a strain.

The first evening she was home they had a gelatin dessert with whipped cream. Mrs. Long brought it to the table with a smile. "All legal, Amy. It's diabetic, without sugar or fat, and it tastes as good as the regular kind; I tried it."

It did taste good, but Jan spoiled it for Amy when she asked, "Are we going to have to have this kind of dessert forever? Can't we ever have chocolate cake and ice cream and apple pie any more?"

I've got diabetes forever, Amy thought resentfully. What was she supposed to do while everybody else ate apple pie with ice cream?

"No, we'll have some of our favorite desserts," Mrs. Long said, with an apologetic glance toward Amy. "But at least part of the time we'll have things we can share with Amy. Lots of them are very good-tasting, and probably better for all of us than too much sugar, anyway."

"Yuck," Jan said, "I don't think that's fair."

"Do you think it's fair I have diabetes?" Amy asked, not even trying to mask her anger.

"Well, no, but what good is it going to do the rest of us to give up everything we like to eat?" Jan demanded, lower lip quivering. "We don't have diabetes. So why should we have to suffer, too?"

At that point Mrs. Long intervened. "That's enough, Jan. We realize we have some problems to work out, but let's not make it harder on everybody than it has to be, okay? All Amy has to give up are the things that are loaded with sugar. I bought a diabetic cookbook, and I've already tried some of the recipes that have less sugar. Dr. Rosenbaum says Amy'll be able to eat everything else she's always had."

Amy didn't really see how it was hard on anybody but *her*. Matt winked at her, but she couldn't summon enough sense of humor to grin back at him. Having diabetes wasn't going to be any fun, and the least her family could do, she thought, was to realize that and sympathize with her.

The dietitian had said Amy wouldn't have to measure out or weigh her portions of each food, the way a few kids had to do, but she was supposed to maintain the proper balance among the different kinds of foods. The carbohydrates were things like bread and cereal and potatoes and vegetables and fruits; the proteins were meat, eggs, fish, poultry,

124

and cheese; the fats were butter, salad dressings, cooking oil, nuts or seeds, and olives; peanut butter was part protein and part fat.

Besides those things, some of each group to be eaten every day, there was a list of "freebies." These were things that she could eat whenever she liked without worrying about how they would affect her blood sugar.

It was Jan who read the list aloud as she stood before the refrigerator where it was posted. "Asparagus, broccoli, brussels sprouts, cabbage, cauliflower, celery, cucumbers, eggplant, green beans, greens—"

"Shut up!" Amy said crossly, but her sister ignored her.

"—Lettuce, mushrooms, okra, peppers, radishes, sauerkraut, spinach, sprouts, summer squash, tomatoes— Boy, I'm glad *I'm* not on this diet!"

"Cut it out, Jan," Matt said.

"There are so many of those things I hate! Amy doesn't like a lot of them, either!"

"Well, don't make it any worse on her," Matt advised.

"But okra? That's that slimy stuff, isn't it? And Amy hates brussels sprouts, too. How is she going to eat those?"

"It doesn't say she has to eat all those," Matt pointed out. "It says they're are good for her, and you've left off things like corn and potatoes and peas and carrots—she *loves* those. Besides, if you can't eat the things you like, you learn to like what you *can* eat. Now knock it off, Jan."

It should have made Amy feel better to know that Matt wanted to be helpful, but what could he do? She was stuck with diabetes no matter what.

The dietician had printed out a sample meal plan for her, showing the approximate balance among the food groups for each meal, and there were suggestions for snacks. Only the snacks weren't what she was used to.

"Carrot strips, apples and oranges, bananas, crackers and cheese—"

No chocolate on the list. After Ginny had told her about the homemade chocolates, Amy had checked with Mrs. Rose to make sure.

"It isn't the chocolate in itself that's bad for you," she'd been told. "It's because most things made with chocolate have a lot of sugar. If you can make candy or desserts without sugar, or with very little of it—there are several good sugar substitutes available now—you can occasionally have chocolate. So sure, go ahead and make something for a special treat. Just eat it in small amounts, and not every day, and it's a good idea to eat your treat on top of a full meal, especially one with lots of fiber. Foods high in fiber slow down the absorption of the glucose into your blood, so you don't run up high blood sugars."

126

Amy hadn't had the courage to ask how often she could have that kind of treat. She already knew they recommended having ice cream—a scant half cup, and plain flavors without topping at that, instead of her favorites combinations—only once or twice a week. What on earth was she supposed to eat the rest of the time?

Even bread, which she loved, was tricky to work in when she couldn't have as much jelly on it as she liked, unless the jelly was sweetened without sugar. Nothing but dietetic syrup on her pancakes, and a sugar substitute on her cereal.

Mrs. Long tried, that first week, to cook foods that Amy could eat as readily as everyone else. One night, though, she sat eating her diet apple crisp with one small scoop of ice cream on it while everyone else loaded up and Jan even had chocolate syrup on hers. Tears stung Amy's eyes.

Going out with Pudge—and most of the time Natalie as well—was even worse. The first time Pudge asked her to go to the Dairy Queen, Amy gave her a direct look.

"What for?" she asked. "I can't eat anything good."

Pudge flushed, then said, "Well, they have diet pop. And . . . and . . ."

"And what?" Amy asked. "It wouldn't be much fun to sit and watch the rest of you wolfing sundaes."

Mrs. Long overheard that exchange. "Honey, they

told us you could have hamburgers and French fries, or a couple of slices of pizza. There are plenty of things you can eat, even an ice cream cone; just stay away from too much of it and don't have fancy toppings that are loaded with sugar. Go on with the girls and have fun."

The trouble was, Amy didn't feel it was that much fun. She didn't want to be the only one who wasn't having what she really wanted. When she watched Pudge eat a tin roof sundae, smothered in butterscotch sauce—Pudge always had butterscotch tin roofs, while Amy had always had chocolate—with peanuts and whipped cream and a cherry on top, her resentment grew.

When Pudge looked up and saw Amy's face as she took the last spoonful—she'd saved the cherry and a glob of whipped cream for last—she flushed.

"You make me feel guilty, eating this in front of you," she said.

Amy's voice was stolid. "I guess I can't expect my friends to give up treats just because I can't have them. My family doesn't."

Pudge got even redder, and then she said, "Why not? Well, no kidding, we're best friends, aren't we? I'll tell you what, when we're eating out, I won't eat anything you can't have! I mean it, Amy! I care enough to want to help you do what you have to do! What do you think, Natalie?"

For a moment Natalie hesitated. She was having

128

a banana split. "Well, sure, if that will make it easier. Maybe we better start walking over to Wendy's, though; they have a salad bar."

For a moment Pudge looked horrified, though she quickly recovered. It was Amy who put the thought into words.

"Some fun, huh? The salad bar." She didn't mention that she didn't have to be *that* strict about what she ate; it gave her an odd, perverse sort of satisfaction to act as if she were being severely deprived. She *felt* deprived.

On the way home, Amy didn't talk much. She felt the tears forming in her eyes. Life wasn't going to be much fun from now on, she could see that.

14.

$\mathbf{W}$hen Amy's Medic Alert bracelet came, she had mixed feelings about putting it on.

It had her name and an identification number, plus a telephone number to call in an emergency. "The people who make the I.D. tags keep a record of important information that's too lengthy to engrave on the tag itself," Ed had told her. "So if anything happens to you, a phone call will get it to any medical personnel who need to know how to treat you."

"It's neat," Pudge said when she saw it. "My uncle has one because he's allergic to penicillin. Yours is nicer, though. Is it silver?"

"Sterling silver," Amy confirmed. The bracelet

felt strange on her wrist. "Dad told Mom to order the nicest one. I don't know if I'm going to wear it to school or not, though."

Pudge stared at her in astonishment. "Why not?"

"Because then everybody will know I'm diabetic," Amy said.

"Well, that's why you get it, isn't it? So anybody will know what to do if you get sick or something. Besides, you aren't going to be able to keep it a secret, Amy. It's not like it's catching, or something to be ashamed of."

"It makes me different," Amy said in a low voice. "I don't want to be different."

She wore the bracelet, though. Because she had an experience that made her see the need for it.

She and Pudge and Natalie had gone skating at the rink. It felt great to be moving fast, flying around the rink to the music with the other kids. For the moment it was as if the diabetes had never happened; she was normal again.

It was so much fun she didn't pay much attention to the time. It wasn't until she began to feel sort of odd that she remembered: they had come to the rink before it was time for her afternoon snack, and she'd forgotten about eating anything. They'd told her to eat *before* she got into strenuous exercise, only it hadn't been long after lunch so she hadn't thought it would matter not to. And then she'd kept on skating, laughing and joking with the other kids,

and the time had gone by so swiftly she hadn't even looked at the clock.

Amy rolled to a stop at one end of the rink, reaching out for the bar to hold herself up. All of a sudden it was scary. She had broken out in a sweat, and she was weak and trembling.

"Amy? What's wrong?" Natalie came up behind her. "Are you sick?"

For a moment Amy's mouth was so dry she couldn't speak. The awful sensations were getting worse, and she realized her Life Savers were in her purse, on a bench at the opposite end of the rink.

"I need some sugar," she said, almost in a croak. "Or some pop—real pop, not diet."

She wasn't sure her knees were going to hold her up; she gripped the railing harder, wondering if she could get to the opening that would get her off the floor to a bench where she could sit down.

"Amy?" Pudge was there, too, her face anxious. "What's happening?"

Panic rolled over her as Amy struggled to stay on her feet. Keep the Life Savers handy all the time, they'd said, but she'd never dreamed she wouldn't be able to get from one end of the rink to the other to get them.

A boy stood on the other side of the rail drinking a Pepsi, and Natalie reached out and snatched it from his hand. "Sorry, my friend's sick and she needs this," she said, and thrust the icy can at Amy.

"Hey, what—?" Luckily the boy didn't grab it back, but watched as Amy drank. At first it was an effort, and then she calmed down a little as the sweet soda went down her throat.

"She's diabetic," Pudge explained to the boy. "We'll pay you for the pop. She needs something with sugar in it."

He looked uncertain. "You sick enough I should ask the manager to call an ambulance or something?" he wanted to know.

"No," Amy managed, draining the can. "Just . . . let me sit down for a minute." The panic was draining away, too. Ed had said to drink something sweet, and rest a minute, and she'd be okay.

With Pudge on one side and Natalie on the other, Amy let them guide her to a bench. She was wobbly, but no longer quite so frightened.

"How long does it take to work?" Natalie wanted to know.

"Not very long. Go ahead and skate," Amy told her.

"No, we'll wait until you're better," Pudge said. "Shall I go get your purse?"

"I'll stay with her," Natalie offered. She dug into the pocket of her jeans. "Here," she said to the boy who was still standing near by, watching. "To pay for the pop."

He shrugged, refusing to take her coins. "Forget it. You okay now?" he addressed Amy.

She nodded. "Maybe I'd better eat something, though."

Within ten minutes she was improved enough so they went over to the food counter and bought hamburgers. By the time they walked home, it was as if nothing had happened.

But the episode had been frightening. From now on, she'd keep the Life Savers in her pocket when she was exercising. And she'd wear the bracelet, too, in case something like this happened when she wasn't with her friends.

The summer was drawing to a close, and it was nearly time for school to start. Unlike everybody else she knew, Amy didn't have to have new clothes because she'd grown out of her old ones, though Ed had told her she'd probably start growing again before long. Gram finished the sweater, and it was beautiful. Mrs. Long bought Amy a white blouse and a brown skirt to go with it, and also two pairs of jeans; Amy hadn't grown out of her old ones, just worn them out.

She was, she supposed, getting somewhat used to the insulin shots before breakfast in the morning and before supper in the evening. Jan refused to stay in the room with her when she gave the shots. Amy didn't really want anyone to watch, to see how she had to psych herself up to do it; yet a part of her resented the aversion Jan obviously felt. If *she* had to do it twice a day, the least Jan could do was learn to accept it as something routine, not disgusting.

Yet much as she disliked injecting herself with the insulin, after the first couple of weeks Amy decided she'd rather do it than have her mother give it to her, when it had to be injected into sites she couldn't reach very well. At least when she did it herself she had control over when it happened.

Matt surprised her one morning when he appeared in the bathroom door as she was carefully drawing the insulin into the needle. "Maybe it would be a good idea if I learned to give the shots, too," he said. "Just in case you're sick or something, sometime."

For a moment Amy didn't think he was serious. "You want to give shots?"

Matt shrugged. "Wouldn't be a bad idea to know how. Who knows, maybe I'll have to take them someday, too. I'd get a head start on the problem, right?"

Amy had wondered bitterly why diabetes had happened to her rather than to anyone else she knew, but it was a shock to think about her brother getting it. "You won't be diabetic," she said. "It's not catching."

"No, but I got the same genes from Mom and Dad as you did. So if that's where it came from, there's a chance I'll turn up with it too, some day.

Or if it's a virus, or a failure of my immune system, that could happen to anybody. On the other hand, I now know how to eat to help prevent diabetes when I'm older. Anyway, why don't you show me how to do it? Just in case?"

It wasn't until she'd finished the procedure that it dawned on Amy that for the first time she'd been thinking of something other than how it was going to hurt, and she'd barely felt the prick of the needle.

Matt was nodding. "Nothing to it. Next time, let me actually do it, okay?"

"Okay," Amy agreed. And when Matt had gone off to run with his friend Jason, she was really glad she had him for a brother.

That evening, when he asked her if she'd like to make a couple of turns around the school track with him, she opened her mouth to say she was too tired and then suddenly realized she wasn't tired at all.

"Okay," she agreed, and wasn't sure who was more surprised, she or Matt.

She only got around the track once before she was winded, but Matt slapped her on the back with an exuberant "Congratulations! That was good, Amy-Janey! Come with me every day, and you'll soon be running fast enough to make the track team!"

"I don't want to make the track team," Amy said, but she was grinning.

"Let's check your blood sugar and see if it's low

enough so you can have a milkshake. You didn't already have any ice cream today, did you?"

She shook her head. "No. But Mom said I'd better not eat it alone on an empty stomach."

"Check your blood sugar and see."

So she did, and they went to the Dairy Queen for the shakes.

Then he made her run again on the way home, and when she checked her blood sugar the next time it was right where it was supposed to be.

"Boy," she said, "I guess I'll have to run, so I can eat more of what I want."

After that, she ran with Matt at least once a day. Her legs got stronger, her wind got better, and she could do a lap and a half around the track by the time school opened. She didn't mind sprawling on the grass, panting, while Matt finished out the second lap, and she always kept her Life Savers in her pocket.

One day she was absorbed in watching Matt—several girls his own age sat in the bleachers watching him, too—when a voice said, "I've seen you running for the past few days. You going to try out for the team this year?"

Amy looked up and nearly choked. It was Danny Crowell, swinging his pitcher's glove in one hand.

Her throat closed and then she got it under control. "Uh, I don't know yet. I'm probably not good enough," she said.

"You looked pretty good just now," Danny said, and walked on to join his friends, leaving Amy looking after him, stunned.

When Matt got back to her, she was feeling so good she was ready to run all the way home.

15.

The Saturday before school started, Amy went with Pudge and Natalie to the ball game in the park. Danny Crowell would be pitching, and this game would decide who took first place. The final game for the county championship would be played the following Saturday, before baseball gave way to soccer and football games.

Natalie wore an air of excitement, and Amy finally demanded, "Who are you going to see?"

"What?" Natalie asked, blushing, and then Pudge laughed.

"Tom Lowry said 'hi' to her in the Easy Supermarket yesterday. She hopes he'll speak to her again at the game."

Tom Lowry was the Blues' best hitter. Amy knew who he was, a tall, attractive boy. Not Danny Crowell, she thought thankfully, though that was silly; Danny was older than they were, and lots of girls thought he was cute.

Both girls had been impressed by Amy's detailed recital—brief though it was—of what Danny had said to her that evening by the track. To have a boy single her out for attention was a first in their group. A feather in Amy's cap, as Gram would have put it.

There were quite a few kids there to watch the game, and a few adults. The girls climbed to the top row of the bleachers and found seats, sharing a big bag of popcorn from the vendor at the edge of the park.

It was a fast, even game. Both teams fought hard, and the score was six to six at the end of the fifth inning when Amy said, "I'm thirsty. I'm going after some pop. Anybody else want some?"

Natalie requested a Coke and Pudge an Orange Crush. Amy worked her way through the crowd to the refreshment stand and bought the canned pop. She was glad that practically everybody sold diet pop as well as the regular kind, and nobody asked why she drank it. A man just ahead of her bought two cans of diet pop, and she wondered if he was diabetic or just watching his weight. Or maybe he liked the taste of it. What Ginny had said was true:

once you got used to it, you couldn't tell the difference.

When she headed back toward the bleachers, there was a knot of noisy boys wrestling right where she needed to walk to get back to her seat. One of them jostled her so that she dropped the pop and then someone else stepped on her fingers while she was picking it up. Stupid kids, she thought, annoyed.

Maybe it would be easier to go around behind the bleachers and hand the pop up to Pudge and Natalie, and then work her way past the boys without trying to juggle three cans in two hands.

Amy retreated and walked behind the bleachers. From here she could see mostly feet and legs in jeans; she tipped her head back and kept walking until she spotted Pudge's new red and white Nikes swinging free.

On the playing field, the umpire called, "Ball four!" and a collective groan ran through the fans. And then, in the relative silence that followed, she heard Natalie's voice.

"Hurry up, before Amy comes back."

Amy's own words died in her throat. She stared upward just as a crumpled candy bar wrapper drifted downward from the stands. A Big Block Hershey. She could smell the chocolate even if she hadn't recognized the wrapper.

A moment later, Pudge said, "Hey, don't throw your trash on the ground—"

She bent over and looked down . . . and saw Amy.

It was hard to say which of them was the more stricken.

Amy sounded as if she'd just swallowed a walnut and her throat hurt. "Here's your pop."

"Oh, gosh, Amy, we didn't know you were there—"

"I could tell," Amy said. She felt betrayed and angry and hurt all at the same time. She handed up the Coke and the Orange Crush and, still clutching her own diet pop, which she no longer wanted, turned and strode away.

She heard Pudge call after her. "Amy, wait, don't be mad, we were just having a chocolate fit, and we didn't want to eat it in front of you—"

"Amy, come back!" Natalie added, but Amy kept on walking.

She bumped into someone, apologized, and ignored the shouts behind her. She walked out of the park, and then ran all the way home.

This was the way it was going to be for the rest of her life, she thought. A part of her mind admitted it was unreasonable to expect everybody she knew to give up candy because she couldn't have it, but she was bitterly disappointed in Pudge. Pudge had offered to go on the diet with her. Well, to refrain from eating sweets when they were together, Amy amended with a touch of honesty. No doubt it was

142

unreasonable to expect someone who wasn't diabetic to give up all her own treats.

Yet Amy's feelings were hurt. She felt isolated and alone. She didn't want to talk to anyone else; she walked quietly past the door of the living room where her dad was reading the paper and her mom and Gram were talking, and up the stairs, hoping Jan wasn't there. She couldn't even have any privacy when she was miserable, she thought, and knowing that made her more miserable than before.

Jan wasn't in the room, but her side of it was a mess. Clothes on the floor, two pair of shoes dropped carelessly, an apple core balanced on the edge of the stand between the beds—*her* night stand as well as Jan's, Amy thought angrily, knocking the apple core into the wastebasket. It wasn't bad enough that she couldn't be alone when she wanted to be, unless she was just lucky and Jan had gone somewhere else, she also had to live with a slob.

She hadn't cried, not in the hospital when they'd told her she'd have diabetes for the rest of her life, nor after she'd come home and had to start giving herself shots and taking blood tests three or four times a day. She felt like crying now.

Amy flung herself on the bed before she realized there was something there beneath her; fury rose inside her, and Amy lifted her body to shove whatever it was off on the floor. How dare Jan put stuff

143

on her bed? She was supposed to stay on her own side of the room, and keep her junk there, too.

It wasn't anything of her sister's, though; Amy realized that as the sheaf of pamphlets cascaded onto the floor. She stared at them through a blur of tears, then looked at the one still under her hand. *American Diabetes Association*, it said.

Something her mother must have picked up and left for her. Amy started to push the last pamphlet over the edge with the rest of them; she was in no mood to think about diabetes. All she wanted to do was pretend she was normal again, like everyone else, and not some freak.

The tears stung her eyes, and she read the title of the little pamphlet through a blur.

ANGER: A Message to the Adolescent with Diabetes.

Anger? The word echoed in Amy's mind. She was angry, all right. Angry at the whole world, for making her have diabetes when other people didn't have to have it.

A wet drop fell on the green paper. *Anger.*

Abruptly, Amy sat up and opened the pamphlet.

A Message to the Adolescent with Diabetes, she read. Well, that was Amy, all right.

She didn't intend to read the rest of it. But her eyes kept following the words, because the rest of them applied to her, too.

When one is said to be "adjusting nicely" to his

144

diabetes, it usually means he's succeeded in hiding his anger from public view.

Amy brushed her eyes with the back of one hand. She drew her legs up and sat cross-legged on the bed, reading.

But hiding anger is like taping up leaks in an old garden hose. Just when you get the problem solved in one place, it pops up in another spot and never really goes away.

That part was true, she thought, swallowing the lump in her throat. She'd thought her close friends— Pudge, at least—would help her, would make it easier. Yet there was Pudge, sneaking a candy bar with Natalie the minute Amy was out of sight.

So what can you do with anger? There are several nonproductive alternatives. One that's popular is getting mad at your doctor (or all doctors). If your doctor is supposed to be such a great healer, you wonder, why doesn't he get busy and cure you? Probably because he studied medicine, not magic. It's hard to apply knowledge that doesn't exist as yet. On the other hand, if you feel he hasn't given you the care and information you need for the daily management of your diabetes, talk to him about it. If this isn't satisfactory, get another doctor. Remember, you're also a consumer.

But that was the trouble, Amy thought in despair. She didn't want another doctor. Dr. Rosenbaum was doing the best he could, she knew that. What made her *furious* was that nobody knew anything to do, and that this had happened to her!

In spite of herself, she kept reading.

Sometimes it's tempting to direct your anger at your parents. After all, diabetes often has strong hereditary characteristics. But you know your parents didn't order a baby with brown eyes, curly hair and diabetes. Being angry with them doesn't make much sense. If things like diet and testing are still a hassle, try a little fresh air here, too. Discuss your problems. Anger over diabetes comes double to parents, believe it or not. Make sure you're not taking out your mutual frustrations on each other.

"What frustrations?" Amy wondered aloud. *She* was the one who had to take shots and blood tests, to eat her meals on time or get sick, to remember to eat before she ran hard, to give up the sugar.

"Talking to yourself?"

Amy jerked her head upward, mortified that Matt had caught her with tears on her cheeks. She swiped at them with the palm of one hand.

"Is there a law against it?" she asked coldly.

"Not that I know of," Matt said cheerfully, advancing into the room and sinking onto the other bed. "You said something about frustrations. You having a bad day?"

"All my days are bad," Amy said, and at the moment she felt it was true.

146

"But today's worse than usual? What's this?" Matt reached over and picked up the pamphlet.

"Something Mom got, I guess." Amy sniffed, then groped for a tissue. "It says parents are frustrated, too. But it's *me* who has diabetes."

Matt's eyebrows went up. "And you think they aren't frustrated? For Pete's sake, Amy, have you looked at them lately?"

"What have they got to be frustrated about?" She sounded sulky, and though she was ashamed, she didn't care enough to apologize.

"Maybe the size of the hospital bills and the cost of the insulin and the needles and the stuff to do your blood tests. That's not all covered by insurance, you know," Matt told her quietly. "And it's expensive."

Startled, Amy looked at him. "Is it?"

"You bet. Dad said he doesn't know how people manage the expense if their insurance doesn't take care of most of it."

A little of her anger slipped away, though not all of it. "Well, I'm sorry, but that's nobody's fault, is it? And it's still *me* who has diabetes. Nobody really understands how hard it is." The tears formed again, and she blinked them away.

"Don't they? Is that why Mom bawled her eyes out the first night she came home from the hospital, after we took you in by ambulance? She wasn't crying about the expense then, she didn't even know what it was going to be, yet. She cried and cried, scared Jan and me, to tell you the truth. Why would she cry, except that she was concerned about you? Because she does understand what it means to have diabetes.''

"She did?'' Amy asked slowly, but she was remembering the way her mother's eyes had looked, red and swollen, the following day.

"Yeah. And Dad reminded her what Dr. Rosenbaum said. That if the parents are strong about it, the kid will handle it better. If the parents fall apart, the kid will freak out, too. So Mom really tried hard to be strong, so it would help you be strong enough.''

"Like Joan,'' Amy said unwillingly. "She didn't want to learn to give herself shots, so her mother agreed to do it.''

"Sometimes,'' Matt said, and she guessed he was quoting their father, "it's easier, in the long run, to be tough at first to help your child learn to be strong.''

She'd never thought of it that way. To be truthful, she didn't want to think of it that way now. She wanted to be left alone with her misery.

Matt stood up, though, and reached out a hand. "Come on. Go for a run with me.''

"I don't feel like running.''

Matt picked up the pamphlet and opened it. "I read this thing, too. And it says, right here—''

Amy swatted it out of his hand. "All right, all

148

right! Forget it! I'd rather run than listen to any more lectures!"

Matt grinned. "Good. I'd rather run than give them. How's your blood sugar? Do you need something to eat before we run?"

Reluctantly, yet feeling some of her anger sliding away, Amy rose from the bed. She couldn't cry in private, so she might as well go with Matt. Maybe it would make her feel better, at least for a little while.

16.

When they sat down to rest for a minute before they headed for home, Matt picked a blade of grass and chewed on it thoughtfully. "You want to tell me what set you off this afternoon? I mean, you've been doing pretty good, as far as I could tell."

Amy was beginning to feel a little ashamed of herself by now. She didn't want to look her brother in the face. "I don't know if I'm ever going to get used to having diabetes, with everybody else around me being able to do what they want."

He regarded her coolly. "Is that how you see it? Everybody else gets to do what they want?"

"Well, don't they?"

"You think that's why Gram's hobbling around

with a walker?" Matt asked. "Because she likes it?"

"I didn't mean that. She got hurt, and she's going to get better."

"Joe Norton has asthma, and it probably isn't going to get any better," Matt said. "Makes it hard for him to play basketball. Impossible to play on the team. He was really hoping to be on the team this year, but his asthma's too bad." Matt stretched out on the grass with his hands under his head, looking up through the leaves of a maple tree. "Joe's brother has planned on being a cop ever since he was in sixth grade and saw the cops intercept a drunk driver who nearly ran him down. But his eyes aren't good enough. He can't pass the test."

For a moment the shame got worse, but then her anger flared again. "That's not the same as having diabetes. He can still do other things."

"Not the things he wants," Matt said softly. "Amy, nobody can do whatever he wants, not all the time. People aren't smart enough to pass the tests for the jobs they want, or they don't have enough talent to sing or dance or act, so they can be in the movies or on TV. Or their health isn't good enough so they can climb mountains or be competitive athletes. They just have to learn to do what they *can* do, and make the best of it. Some of them become the best there is, in their second choice."

"If that's supposed to make me feel better," Amy

said, her voice muffled as she buried her face on her drawn-up knees, "it isn't working."

"What happened?" Matt asked, still very quietly so the kids playing on the swings a short distance away wouldn't hear.

In a burst of emotion, she told him. "And I came back and they were eating a Big Block bar."

For a moment Matt didn't say anything, until Amy lifted her head and stared at him.

Then his words were mild. "What did you expect them to do? Eat it in front of you?"

Amy flushed. "No! But Pudge said she'd stay on the diet with me—"

"When she was with you, right? She said she wouldn't eat hot fudge sundaes in front of you, didn't she? Not that she'd never eat one again, ever."

"But they *were* with me, they knew I'd be back in a few minutes—"

"And they were trying to finish eating it before you got there. They didn't mean to hurt you. They were trying *not* to hurt you. Weren't they?"

She stared at him through blurred eyes. "I hate having diabetes! I hate it, *I hate it*, I HATE IT!"

"I'll bet all diabetics hate it. All twelve million of 'em."

"They don't all know they have it," Amy said perversely. "Not all of them have even been diagnosed yet."

"Well, that makes you one of the lucky ones, doesn't it?"

Her jaw dropped. "How do you figure that?"

"Because you know what made you sick, and you know what to do about it." He sat up, then leaped to his feet, reaching down to grab her hand. "Come on. Time to run home."

She was pretty well winded when they got there. Her mother was in the kitchen making salad, and something smelled wonderful.

"Spare ribs?" Amy asked hopefully. "Barbecued ribs?"

"Right. Set the table for me, will you? Oh, and Amy, Pudge has called twice. She sounded urgent. Did you two have a fight or something?"

"Not really," Amy said. "I'll call her."

Her mother smiled and brushed a kiss across her temple. "Good. Pudge is your best friend, and she cares, honey, even if you do have an occasional misunderstanding."

Pudge answered the phone on the first ring. "Amy? Look, we didn't think you'd know! I'm sorry—"

"It's okay," Amy interrupted. Part of what Matt had been saying had sunk in, and she had to admit she wasn't being fair to her friend. "I *was* upset, but it's because of me—what I can't do, can't have."

"We didn't want to make you upset," Pudge said. "Honest, I've hardly had any candy since you got sick. I still want it, too, but I look at it and feel guilty."

"You don't need to," Amy said. "I do appreciate it, that you don't eat it in front of me, though."

"I won't, ever," Pudge said earnestly. "And if Natalie brings any more candy bars along, I'll turn it down when she offers it to me."

Again the tears prickled behind Amy's eyelids. "We've been friends a long time. I don't want us not to be friends."

"Neither do I," Pudge said. "Listen, did you write any more on the story about the dragon? I'm drawing a picture of one, and I want you to see if it's good enough to illustrate your story."

"I'll be over after supper," Amy offered, "and take a look. I'm sure it's good. Everything you draw is fantastic."

She was right. Pudge was in her room when Amy got there, with the work spread out on her desk. The dragon was a brilliant green, with red flames coming out of his mouth.

"He's gorgeous," Amy said truthfully, and Pudge blushed with pleasure.

Mrs. Rapinchuck appeared in the doorway. "You girls want a snack? I got some really nice apples today."

They each took one, crunching away while Amy explained how she was going to end the dragon story and Pudge finished her drawing. Amy walked home later through the dusk, no longer angry, only sad. She still had diabetes. There was no way to make it go away.

This time Jan was in their room. When Amy kicked a tennis shoe out of the way, under her sister's bed, Jan got a tight look around the mouth.

"I'm not the only one making a mess," the younger girl said. "How come you threw all that stuff on the floor?"

"I felt like it," Amy said, but she bent over to retrieve the pamphlets her mother had brought home from the American Diabetes Association office. She started to drop them into the wastebasket, then hesitated and put them on the nightstand instead.

Later, after she'd taken her bath and put on her pajamas, she sat up in bed and picked up the pamphlet she'd been reading when Matt came in.

There's not much help I can give when it comes to brothers and sisters, she read. *It is obviously unfair for you to have diabetes while they get off free. Resentment is reasonable in this situation. But what are you going to do with the anger? Everyone fights with his siblings now and then. Diabetes is no worse than some other excuses for fighting, but how does it help you?*

Jan suddenly turned on her radio, full blast, to the kind of music Amy couldn't stand. Amy leaned far over to pick up another of the tennis shoes off the floor and threw it.

Jan yelped and turned around. "You cut that out! That hurt, Amy Jane Long! I *hate* you!"

Amy bit her lip. Like the pamphlet said, what good had that done?

"I'm sorry. I didn't know I could throw well enough to hit you. I just meant to get your attention and tell you to turn down the volume."

Jan glared. "I'm right in the same room. I could have heard you if you'd just asked. Politely."

For a few seconds Amy boiled inwardly, and then she said, in a meek enough tone, "I'm sorry. Please turn down the volume; it's giving me a headache."

Jan didn't answer, but she turned down the music. Amy went on reading.

As far as the rest of the world is concerned, you'll find your diabetes is a lonely disease. Because your diabetes is not obvious to other people, they won't give you much help or support or even sympathy. Sometimes this is a great blessing, but at those times when you feel you need a little understanding and you don't get it, you may become furious.

Boy, that was no lie, Amy thought.

Caring for diabetes is like tinkering with a short wave radio or a very old car. You never finish the project. Even when your diabetes is not giving you trouble, it's just plain boring. It always needs attention, seven days a week, 365 days a year, no vacations, no days off. Who wouldn't want to go up

156

on a mountain top and shout, "I hate it!" every once in a while?

I do hate it, Amy thought. I hate it, *hate it*, HATE IT!

There is no answer for coping with the anger, she read. *You are as individual as a thumbprint, and you're going to have to find a solution to the problem that is custom-tailored to you. But just realizing there is a problem is a great step forward.*

Just as she'd figured. The pamphlet didn't offer any easy solutions. It just told her it was *her* problem. She'd already known that, but she kept on reading.

Anger comes in big and little waves. Sometimes it helps just to relieve the pressure. Crying is good for this. I used to do a lot of crying in the shower. That way you don't make puddles, and you get clean, too.

Why, whoever wrote this must be a diabetic, too. It made Amy feel strange, that someone with similar problems had written this material. It wasn't the same as if it had been written by a doctor, or someone else who didn't really understand.

Hard, grubby, physical work is very therapeutic. So is exercise. It doesn't matter if it's tennis, karate, football, or jumping rope, as long as you are busy turning anger into perspiration. Sometimes when you're coping with frustration, the choice seems

157

to be eating or exercise. Try to choose exercise. You'll have fewer regrets the next day.

There are quiet ways to handle anger, too. Prayer, meditation, or a frank discussion with an understanding friend can turn down the heat when you're boiling mad.

Like talking to Matt, Amy realized. He could defuse the situation just by being there. By pointing out things she hadn't considered, by putting them into perspective. And Ed Soldenski, who had quoted: *I cried because I had no shoes, and then I met a man who had no feet.* It didn't make the diabetes go away, but it made it clear that there might be worse problems than the ones she was dealing with.

On the other hand, the reading went on, *it might be a good idea to get mad and stay mad until it does some good. Consider your anger raw energy. Harness it and use it as a weapon to slay the dragon diabetes.*

Amy didn't quite understand that part. She frowned and went on.

One young man wrote me of his unhappiness with inadequate medical care, legislation, educational materials, etc., and wondered where to place the blame. He concluded that people with diabetes get exactly what they ask for and urged them to band together and develop a generation of diabetics with backbones who are willing to help themselves and each other. He has a good point.

158

Amy's frown deepened. She didn't quite understand all of that, either. Her own medical care was good—at least she thought it was—and she didn't know what legislation had to do with having diabetes. She'd talk to her father, she decided, and maybe he could explain that part. What the writer said about having the backbone to help themselves and each other sort of tied in with Ed telling them they'd have to be aggressive enough to get what they needed, didn't it?

"Is it okay with you if I leave the radio on, real low, for a while?" Jan asked.

"What? Oh, sure. Just so it's not loud," Amy agreed. She turned off her light and lay back on the pillows.

It hadn't been the greatest day she'd ever had, and she suspected there were some more bad ones coming up—when she went back to school, for instance—but maybe she'd made some progress.

It was all right to cry, the writer had said.

It was funny, but after she'd read that, she hadn't felt like crying anymore. Not for now, anyway.

17.

Normally, after a summer's vacation, Amy was eager to go back to school. This year was different; she would be moving up to junior high, and she had diabetes.

The junior high part was exciting, though a little scary. She'd only gone to one school before, and everything this year would be new. Except, of course, that the kids would be the same, and some of them she hadn't seen since last spring.

A few days before school opened, Amy got dressed and stared in amazement at her jeans, then raced to find her mother, who was making up the bed in her own room.

160

"Mom! Mom, look!"

Mrs. Long gave the bedspread a final tuck and turned toward the doorway. "What's up?"

"Look! My jeans can hardly snap shut! Mom, I'm getting *fatter*!"

Mrs. Long laughed. "Well, I guess you are. Maybe a little taller, too, if those pant legs are any indication."

"I've started to grow again," Amy said in wonder.

"It sure looks like it. Maybe you'd better try on everything you own today, so we know what we'll have to replace. I don't know when we'll get to go shopping, though. Gram's decided she's well enough to give up the walker and go home, so we'll be moving her tomorrow. You'll be getting your room back, and it wasn't so terrible sharing with Jan, was it?"

"It wasn't like having my own room, though. Is Gram sure she's ready to live alone again?"

"Not only to live alone, but she's talking about going back to work, though that's probably a month or so off yet. But she's determined to go on her cruise to Alaska." Mrs. Long gave Amy a hug. "I'm glad you're growing, honey, even if it is going to cost a small fortune to re-outfit you. You've been shortchanged in that department this last year or so."

Before Gram moved out, she gave each member of the family a present. "For being such good sports about having an old lady disrupt your household," she told them. The gifts were nice, but Amy's was the nicest of all.

"Because you're the one who got booted out of her room," Gram said, handing Amy the box, "and because this'll help you keep track of when it's time for blood testing and insulin shots."

The present was a digital watch with a stretchy gold link band. It not only told the time, it gave the date, indicated what time its alarm was set for (just before supper, so she'd be reminded to take her insulin then; she didn't have any trouble remembering the morning shot) and counted out the seconds for her blood testing. Besides that, it beeped gently every hour on the hour, to make her aware of the passing of time.

"It's wonderful!" Amy said, throwing her arms around Gram's neck. "Thank you!"

It seemed peculiar to be back in a room by herself again when Gram had gone. Peculiar, but nice. When Pudge came over, they could giggle and talk without whispering. And she wouldn't have to listen to Jan's horrid music or her stupid and insensitive remarks.

Pudge couldn't wait to go to school at the junior high. There would be all kinds of school activities that no reasonable parent could object to their attending: sock hops, athletic events, and Pudge had decided to try out for the drama group that met after school two afternoons a week.

162

"Why don't you come, too, Amy? Even if they don't let us act onstage, maybe I could paint scenery, and you're good at writing, they might even let you help do a play!"

That didn't seem likely, but it did sound exciting. Amy agreed to go to the opening meeting, anyway, to see what the possibilities were.

"I've got some money I earned cleaning out the garage," Pudge said. "Let's go ride our bikes, and when it's time for you to eat your snack, it'll be my treat."

They rode aimlessly, effortlessly. Amy could still remember how tired she'd been earlier in the summer, though. How riding a bike or running or even walking very far had been more than she could do. It was a good feeling to have energy again. And if she really was growing, maybe she wouldn't stay the smallest one in the seventh grade.

The watch beeped so softly that sometimes, if she was thinking about something else or in noisy surroundings, she didn't notice it. Riding quietly along Grove Street, though, she heard it sound and realized, at the same time, that the Mini-Mart was right ahead.

"Let's go there and get a snack," Amy suggested. "I met the owner when we were both in the hospital."

Mr. Gambini greeted them with enthusiasm. "Well, it's about time you visited my store! What can I do for you? Ice cream bars? No, I forget, you're diabetic. Apples, then, or bananas? Crackers and cheese? And diet pop, right? Or milk?"

They each chose a big green Granny Smith apple, and Mr. Gambini cut them each a slice of cheese from a huge round in his glass counter. "Have a cracker," he added, opening a box and setting it out as well.

They were having their snack when Coby arrived.

He still needed a haircut, and he still wore faded jeans and worn-out athletic shoes, but he grinned when he saw Amy.

"Well, if it ain't another sugar baby. How you doing?"

"Okay," Amy said. She felt both embarrassed and pleased, and introduced him to Pudge. "How about you? Still playing ball?"

"Yeah. We're gonna take the championship next Saturday," Coby said. Amy had nearly forgotten how arrogant he could be.

"Maybe not," Amy said. "Our team is pretty good."

"Not good enough against this old arm." Coby swung his imaginary bat and looked up toward the ceiling. "See? There it goes, the home run that will win us the game. Come and see it happen."

"Maybe I will," Amy said. She had to smile in spite of herself.

"Bring your handkerchief," Coby said. "Be prepared to cry when your team loses." He reached over and took one of the crackers from the box, then added a bite of cheese. "Staying on your wonderful old diabetic diet, are you?"

"Yes," Amy said. "Are you?"

Coby shrugged, as if it didn't matter. "More or less. What you want me to do today, Mr. Gambini?"

The old man shuffled sideways, awkward in the cast he still wore on his foot. "There's a shipment in the back room. Needs to be opened and put on the shelves."

Coby gave him a mock salute, grinned at the girls, and said, "Got to go to work. See you around."

When he'd disappeared into the rear of the store, Amy looked at Mr. Gambini.

"Is he eating junk he shouldn't have?"

"No. He talks smart-mouth, but he's a pretty good kid," Mr. Gambini said. "I think he wants to get that athletic scholarship; it's the only way he'll ever get to college. He's behaving himself all right, only he can't admit it for fear people will think he's going soft." He smiled at the girls. "Nothing wrong with being a little soft sometimes. Like my missus. She likes Coby. She invites him over to supper a couple times a week, now she's found out what he's supposed to eat. It don't sound like he gets fed at home unless he cooks it himself. You're lucky, young lady. You got folks that care about you."

It was a statement Amy remembered for a long

time. She thought about it when she was feeling sorry for herself, and guilt made her realize that she *was* lucky in many ways.

The first day of school Amy dressed carefully in the new pleated skirt and white blouse. It was too warm to wear the new sweater, but her mother had bought her a bright orange and brown print scarf to wear with the blouse. After today she'd wear jeans a lot of the time, but the first day most of the kids showed off their new outfits.

Pudge was wearing new clothes, too, a blue skirt with a lighter blue top. Amy stopped when she saw her. "Hey! Pudge, are you losing weight? You look positively slim!"

Pudge flushed with pleasure. "Can you tell? I've lost four pounds. Mom says it's because I quit eating so much junk since you've been on a diet. If it wasn't for Natalie and her candy bars, maybe I wouldn't be tempted so much."

"You look great," Amy told her sincerely. "I'm gaining, and you're losing, and maybe we'll both look great. If you keep on getting slimmer, we'll have to stop calling you Pudge."

Pudge got even pinker with delight. "Do you think so? The teachers will all be new this year. If I tell everybody to call me Sylvia, do you think they will?"

"If they don't, we'll hit 'em over the head with our notebooks," Amy suggested, and they giggled as they walked on toward school.

The giggles covered Amy's nervousness until they actually arrived. Then she didn't feel like laughing any more. She had the pamphlets to give to her teachers, but she hated the idea of making herself conspicuous by handing them out. She was wearing her Medic Alert bracelet, hoping nobody would notice it right away, although the news about her diabetes had probably gotten around to a lot of the kids already.

"Hi, Amy! Hi, Pudge!" It was Debbie Orvis, whom they hadn't seen all summer. "I saw your name on the list for Mrs. Small for homeroom. I'm in there, too."

Amy informed her that Pudge was now going to answer only to the name Sylvia, and they went to look at the list. Amy knew Mrs. Small by reputation; Matt had had her in seventh grade and liked her.

There were kids milling around in the hallways, looking at the lists, finding out where to go, greeting each other like long-lost friends. Natalie found them, her face showing disappointment. "I'm in a different homeroom from you two," she said, and Amy felt a small surge of satisfaction. It wasn't that she disliked Natalie, but she wanted to maintain the closer relationship she'd always had with Pudge. That would be easier if they shared a homeroom and Natalie didn't.

A bell rang, and the crowds surged with more purpose. Amy inhaled deeply. "Well, I guess we better go in," she said.

Mrs. Small was youngish and rather pretty. She smiled as Amy approached her desk. "To start with, just take a seat anywhere," she said.

"Yes, ma'am. I'm supposed to give you this," Amy said. Her heart was thudding. What if the teacher decided she didn't want a diabetic kid in her class?

"Aren't you Matt Long's sister?" At Amy's nod, Mrs. Small said, "I thought so. And you're diabetic? Will you need anything, or will you carry your own Life Savers or sugar cubes?"

"I'll carry my own," Amy said, surprised that Mrs. Small knew about that without even glancing at the pamphlet.

"My younger brother is diabetic," Mrs. Small said. "I grew up feeling deprived because our mother wouldn't let the rest of us eat a lot of sugar, either. Now I'm glad she didn't. Welcome to junior high, Amy."

Feeling confused and relieved, Amy took a seat next to Pudge. She hoped the rest of the teachers would be as readily accepting as Mrs. Small.

Actually, she encountered two who didn't know anything about diabetes but were interested in learning, one who actually *had* diabetes, and the others had had diabetic kids in their classes before. After

168

all that worrying, it seemed there was no problem with teachers understanding her situation.

When she retired to the rest room to check her blood sugar, a small knot of girls clustered around her. "What're you doing?" one of them asked.

When she pricked her finger and let the blood settle onto the reagent strip, one of the girls said, "Oh, yuck," but the others were interested. They wanted an explanation, and Amy gave it to them, feeling self-conscious.

"I've got an aunt with diabetes," one of them volunteered. "She doesn't have to take shots, though."

"I know a girl in eighth grade who has diabetes," another one stated. "Come on, there's the bell, let's go."

It was sort of an anticlimax, but Amy felt better. Nobody had treated her as if she were a freak, and she was grateful.

When it came time for her snack, she ate it quietly in class, careful not to crackle wrappers or draw attention to herself. Afterward a boy asked why she was allowed to eat, and she gave him a simple explanation. He nodded as if he found that reasonable, and no more was said.

By the time school was out on the first day, Amy's spirits had risen quite a lot. Enough so that after she left Pudge off at her house, she ran all the way home, eager to work on her new story. She'd already told Pudge the plot, so her friend would be sketching some preliminary pictures to go with it.

It was good to be in the privacy of her own room again. Amy carried her afternoon snack in and sat on her bed with her notebook. For the next few hours, until the alarm went off to remind her, she forgot she had diabetes.

18.

The first week of school went better than Amy had dreamed could be possible. Several people remarked on her Medic Alert bracelet. Most of the kids expressed interest or sympathy; nobody said, "Yuck!" the way Jan had, even when she told them about the shots and the blood tests.

Once Mr. Monahan asked who had the watch alarm that beeped on the hour, but when she told him why she wore it, he simply nodded. Most of the time it went off when the bell was ringing for a change of classes, anyway, and nobody noticed it.

The gym teacher was quite different from Miss Kramer, their former P.E. instructor. Mrs. Jernigan was young and slim and pretty; she enjoyed the girls in her classes, enjoyed what she was teaching them, and though she was pretty shrewd about seeing through flimsy excuses about why a girl couldn't play volleyball or take a shower, she was understanding about everything else.

She nodded when Amy timidly handed her the pamphlet about diabetes. "We have a girl in ninth grade who's diabetic—Mary Susan Deal, do you know her?"

Amy shook her head.

"Well, just keep your snacks handy. I always have orange juice in my office, and I carry sugar cubes, too, in case you don't have them when you need them."

Warmth flooded through Amy as she smiled back. "Thank you," she said. It was a relief to have teachers who knew what she was going through, without having to make detailed explanations.

It was better at school, actually, than it was at home. There were times when Amy thought that if she'd still been sharing a room with Jan, they'd have gotten into some real fights.

Jan seemed to resent everything Amy said or did. It didn't matter that the brownies their mother baked tasted great; they were made partly with a sugar substitute for Amy's benefit, and Jan liked the old recipe better.

"Fine. Make yourself some with the old recipe," Mrs. Long said. Jan only glowered, not complying.

If Amy was on the phone, talking to Pudge, Jan hung around, listening. When Amy objected, her sister said she was waiting for her turn to use the telephone.

When Amy was using the bathroom to prepare her insulin injection, or doing a finger stick for a blood test, Jan complained because she was tying up the bathroom.

"Use the one upstairs," Amy suggested.

"Why should I have to walk all that way every time? Hurry up, Amy."

"I can't hurry. It just takes a few minutes," Amy pointed out, and wondered why Jan had become so disagreeable.

Once, without asking, Jan borrowed her new sweater, the one Gram had made, to go to a movie with her friends. Amy was spending the night with Pudge and wouldn't have known the difference, except that Mr. Rapinchuck took the girls out for a late-evening pizza and Amy saw Jan getting into Susan Balstrom's mother's station wagon.

As soon as they got back to Pudge's house, Amy called home and talked to her mother. "Just because Gram hasn't quite finished *her* sweater doesn't give her the right to take mine without asking!" Amy said indignantly.

"No, it doesn't," her mother agreed, though she didn't sound nearly as upset as Amy was. "We'll have a family discussion about it."

To Amy's further indignation, Jan wasn't even apologetic.

"You weren't wearing it," she said. "And I didn't hurt it."

"But it's *mine*! Don't you know enough to ask before you use other people's belongings?"

"You wouldn't have let me wear it if I'd asked," Jan accused. "Would you?"

"No! And you better not take anything of mine again if you know what's good for you!" Amy replied. "I mean it, Jan, you'll be sorry."

Jan shrugged. "So who cares?"

"Enough, enough," Mrs. Long intervened. "You're sisters. You have to live in the same household for years yet. Let's have some peace and harmony, all right?"

"As long as she stays out of my things," Amy said.

She was unprepared for the flash of bitter animosity in her sister's face.

"It's not fair," Jan said. "Everything around here is for Amy! She gets to stay out later, have the best clothes, she hogs the bathroom, and everything we eat depends on what *Amy* can eat! Nobody cares about me anymore!"

Amy walked off while her mother was dealing with that statement. Matt was sitting on the back step cleaning his Nikes with a toothbrush and detergent suds. "What's going on?"

"Jan's being hateful. As usual," Amy added. "She's a real brat."

"Oh, she's a pretty good kid most of the time," Matt said. "She's just feeling left out since you've become the center of attention in this family."

Amy stared at him in astonishment. "Me? The center of attention?"

"You mean you haven't noticed that you have been, ever since you got sick? Jan missed going to a party that first night. Mom was supposed to drive her there, but she forgot about it when she found out you'd gone to the hospital. And the whole time you were in there, nobody talked about anything but diabetes and how it was going to affect the rest of your life, and what it would mean to the rest of us, too."

Matt finished with one shoe and picked up the other one, working the foam in with the toothbrush. "I don't mind so much if Mom's gone overboard on this healthy food kick. I guess she's right, it is better for us. But she's stopped fixing some of the things we all liked, or is using different recipes so they're better for a diabetic. You can't really blame Jan for feeling left out of the decisions."

"Maybe she'd like to be the one with diabetes," Amy said crossly. "Then she'd understand what it's like."

Matt stopped cleaning his shoe and looked at her. "I think she understands what it's like, Amy."

"How can you say that?" Amy heard her voice rising. Matt was usually pretty sensible, but this time he was off base by a mile. "She resents me for things I can't help, and she keeps going 'yuck' about everything. She doesn't understand, and she doesn't care!"

"Why do you think it bothers her so much, if she doesn't care? She's scared, Amy. She sees Mom and Dad paying more attention to you, and less to her, and she's afraid it's going to be like that forever. That what you need will always be more important than what she needs."

"My diabetes is going to be forever," Amy reminded him.

"Sure. And it scares us. We can't help thinking that maybe we'll get it someday, too. If we didn't understand what it means to you, would we be afraid of it?"

"It's under control now," Amy said. "I'm not having any big problems." It was true, she realized. Except that she still didn't like sticking the needles in herself, she wasn't having any trouble.

"Good. Just give us a little while to forget what it was like when it *wasn't* under control. And try

176

to sympathize with Jan. It hasn't been easy for her, you know, to stop being the baby of the family overnight."

"If she'd stop acting like a baby, it would be easier for everybody," Amy said, still feeling sullen.

"Right." Matt put aside his cleaned shoes. "You going to the championship game tomorrow? It should be a good one."

"Yes, I'm going with Pudge and Natalie. Seems funny to be having a baseball championship when they've already started playing soccer and football."

Matt stood up. "That's what we get when there were too many games rained out this summer. Tell Mom I've gone over to Joe's, will you?"

So that crisis passed. Amy didn't know if Matt was right about Jan or not, but she could understand a little of how her sister felt. Enough so she made an effort to be civil to Jan, if not particularly friendly.

There was a big turnout for the game on Saturday. The parents of the players were there as well as several hundred kids. For once Amy and her friends didn't arrive early enough to sit on the top seat of the bleachers. In fact they wondered for a few minutes if they were going to get into the bleachers at all, they were so full.

Then, as they stood indecisively looking around, four boys rose from the lower seats and left. "Come on," Natalie said quickly, "let's sit there."

"Go ahead, and save me a seat," Amy said. "I

see a friend from the hospital I want to speak to first."

Elizabeth didn't seem as thin as she had been, either. She greeted Amy with a smile. "Come to see Coby hit his winning home run?" she asked.

"We'll see," Amy said, laughing. "He's confident, isn't he?"

Elizabeth looked more confident, too. "How you doing?"

"Good," Amy responded, and knew it was true. "You seen any of the other kids from the hospital?"

"Ginny and Coby, though not very often." Elizabeth sobered. "I went up to the hospital yesterday to see Joan."

Amy's stomach tightened. "Is she back in?"

"Yeah. She won't stay on the diet. She's been in twice since we all got out the first time. Her mom still gives her the shots, and she cheated on her blood testing. Said it was okay when it wasn't, and wrote the wrong figures in her book."

There was a moment of silence between them. "There's a test they do, remember? Ed told us about it. The glycohemoglobin, the one they call the A_{1c} test. It tells what your blood sugar has averaged over the past couple of months, and they found out Joan's had been really high. Her mom was practically in hysterics at the doctor's office."

Amy thought about what her father had said,

when she was in the hospital: that sometimes you had to be tough on your kid at first to make it easier later. "I was scared to death," she said, "but I'm glad they made me learn to give my own shots."

"Me, too. Otherwise I couldn't spend the night away from home or go to camp or anything. Looks like the game's going to start. I'll see you later."

"See you later," Amy echoed. She was glad she'd met Elizabeth, and sorry about Joan. She joined Pudge and Natalie, squeezing in between them.

They had come prepared with popcorn and soda pop. There was a suspicious bulge in the pocket of Natalie's sweat shirt, but Amy decided to ignore it. As long as Natalie didn't eat candy in front of her, she supposed she had to get used to the idea.

It was a lively game. Danny Crowell was pitching for the Blues, as was to be expected in an important game. And for the Cougars, Coby Bonner was playing third base and swinging the Big Bat.

The first two innings, it was three up, three down, on both sides. Then in the third, Coby caught a pop fly that kept the Blues from scoring, and at his own turn at bat he got a double.

When he stole third base, Amy heard herself yelling with the other Cougar fans: "Slide, Bonner, slide!"

"Who you rooting for?" Natalie demanded. "I thought you wanted the Blues to win!"

"Well," Amy said, flustered, "I want everybody I know to do his best."

Coby might brag a lot, but it wasn't idle arrogance. He was good. Amy thought about what she'd been told, that getting an athletic scholarship would be the only way Coby could go to college.

Danny was good, too, but it was a foregone conclusion that he'd go on to college, with or without a scholarship. His mom was a gynecologist and his dad was chief of surgery at the local hospital; they had enough money to send him to any school where he could meet the entrance requirements.

So far Amy hadn't thought much about college. What she wanted to do when she grew up was write stories, maybe starting on a newspaper the way her mother had, and eventually write books, maybe. She didn't know if there were college courses for that or not. But she knew it would be important to most kids to get a good education. Especially a kid like Coby, who didn't have family support for anything, not even his diabetes.

In the fourth inning, the Blues scored a run. They came close to getting a second one, but Coby threw the man out at the plate. The crowd went wild, jumping up and down and screaming.

The Cougar fans clapped and hollered approval. "Way to go, Bonner!" they yelled, and Coby grinned and wiped the sweat off his face, glancing toward the stands.

Amy didn't know if he noticed that she was there. She was wearing a brilliant red shirt, but most of the people around her were in bright colors, too.

In the next inning, the Cougars loaded the bases, with one out. It was their big chance to move ahead. However, the Blues brought the crowd to their feet with a double play: one man scored, but the first baseman picked off a second man, and Danny beat the third one to home plate, to end the inning. The score was tied.

Amy studied all the faces. Every player was intent, eager, keyed up. Most of them wiped their foreheads from time to time, because it was hot.

The score was still one and one in the final inning. The Blues got one man on base, and then three pop flies, easily caught by Coby and a teammate, retired the side.

If the Cougars could get a run, they'd win the championship.

"Bonner, Bonner," the crowd chanted. "Give us the Big Bat!"

Amy held her breath when Coby came to the plate. He swaggered, taking a few practice swings, and then took his stance.

The crowd fell silent. Amy knew who she was rooting for now. "Come on, Coby," she murmured under her breath. "Hit a long one!"

"Ball one!" the umpire bellowed.

Coby grinned, and Danny scowled. Danny went

into his windup and pitched the ball.

The crack was like a rifle shot. Again the crowd was on its feet, screaming. "Run! Run!"

Coby ran for all he was worth. He had a triple easily; the fielders were chasing the ball, relaying it to the infield. Coby hesitated at third, then sprinted for home.

The roar of the crowd was deafening. "Slide! Slide, Bonner!" his fans screamed.

Coby dove for the plate, his outstretched fingers touching the bag only seconds before the ball smacked into the catcher's mitt.

"Safe!" the umpire yelled, and the game was over. The Cougars had won. Cougars fans jumped off the bleachers, hugged each other, danced around.

But Coby was still on the ground. He had been flat; now he got to his hands and knees, but his head was down, he wasn't getting up.

His teammates surrounded him, thumping him on the back, dragging him to his feet. Coby staggered, reaching out to a friend for support.

Some of the tumult died down.

"What's wrong with him?"

"Is he stoned?" someone asked clearly.

And suddenly Amy knew what was wrong. Her mouth was dry, and she stared at the Medic Alert disk dangling from the chain around Coby's neck. Nobody else was paying any attention to it.

Ed Soldenski had said they had to be aggressive when it was necessary, to see that the proper things were done to help themselves. Surely that included helping each other as well.

The Cougar's coach was coming from the side of the field, but Amy was on her feet, too. "Give me your candy bar," she told Natalie, and didn't wait for a response. She grabbed it out of Natalie's sweat shirt pocket—a Mars Bar—and ran toward home plate. She had to push her way through the crowd, breaking through just as Coby sagged to his knees, folding forward.

"They shouldn't let anybody play who can't stay sober," Amy heard a woman's voice say behind her. Why did some people always have to assume the worst?

Amy spoke angrily over her shoulder. "He hasn't been drinking, he's diabetic!" And he'd just run flat out, all the way around the bases, with everything he had, she wanted to add, but she didn't have the breath for it.

She went down on her knees beside Coby. "Here, eat some of this," she urged, tearing off the wrapper and thrusting it into his hand.

Coby's eyes were glazed, but he took a bite. He didn't speak, just nodded and chewed.

The coach had reached the inner circle around them. "Clear away, get back and give the kid some air. He's diabetic, he needs some—oh, he's got candy. Good thinking, girl. How you doing, Bonner?''

Coby sank back onto his heels, nodding. Perspiration poured from his face, and the coach brought out a handkerchief to wipe it off. ''I'll be okay in a few minutes,'' Coby said. ''Guess I overdid it.''

''You won the game,'' Amy said, as tremulous as if it were she herself who had collapsed.

''Told you I would,'' Coby panted, and everybody laughed.

The crowd began to disperse; the coach headed toward the dugout, leaving Amy and Coby still crouched near home plate. He wiped sweat off his forehead, and under his tan she thought he looked pale. He gave her a sheepish glance.

''My own fault,'' he mumbled, looking away. ''I had to work this morning, and I didn't have much time to eat, so I just grabbed a sandwich. It wasn't enough, before a game. Maybe old Vampire Soldinski's right, I get stupid sometimes.''

He still hadn't made any move to get to his feet. She felt conspicuous, standing there beside him. Her mouth was dry when she spoke. ''You all right now?''

He nodded, still looking down into the dirt.

Amy stood uncertainly for a moment, then picked up the candy wrapper and headed for her friends.

''Gosh, that was quick thinking,'' Pudge told her. ''How'd you know Natalie had a candy bar?''

"Guessed," Amy admitted.

"Why didn't you use your own Life Savers?" Natalie wanted to know, though she didn't sound annoyed that her Mars Bar had vanished.

"Never thought of it," Amy confessed, feeling foolish.

"Our team lost the championship," Natalie said.

Amy didn't reply. She didn't feel like one of the losers.

She still didn't when she got home. She felt so good, in fact, that when Jan announced that she was going swimming, but her bathing suit was still wet from the last time and she didn't want to put it on all damp and yucky, Amy offered her own.

"It's getting tight on me, so it shouldn't be too big for you," she said. "And I'm not going swimming today."

Jan stared at her distrustfully, until Amy handed her the suit. "Well, thanks." She stood for a moment, then cleared her throat. "I . . . I wish you were . . . an ordinary healthy person, Amy. I do, honest."

"I am an ordinary healthy person," Amy said. "I just happen to have diabetes."

"Hey, Amy! Telephone!" Matt shouted.

Amy walked out in the hall. "If it's Pudge, tell her—"

Matt was holding his hand over the receiver. "It's

not Pudge. It's some guy. Says he forgot to thank you." Matt made his eyebrows go up, and he was grinning.

Amy reached for the phone, her heartbeat quickening. Wait until she told Pudge and Natalie that she'd had her first phone call from a boy, and the hero of the Cougars, at that.

Amy accepted the receiver. Then she motioned at Jan, who was standing there with her mouth open. "Beat it. This is a private conversation."

Jan shrugged and went away without arguing, for once.

She wouldn't be twelve for nearly six months, but suddenly Amy felt quite grown-up. "Hello?" she said into the phone. "Yes, this is Amy. Oh, hi, Coby."

GLOSSARY

Acetone A waste product formed in the body, usually when there is not enough insulin. It often forms during illness, stress, or after an insulin reaction. Acetone is a warning sign that the diabetes is not as well controlled as it should be. (See *Ketones*.)

Autoimmunity A process in which the immune system in the body turns against the body and attempts to destroy a portion of it. The destruction of the cells that produce insulin is thought to be caused by autoimmunity.

Cells The building blocks of the body. The body contains millions of cells that need insulin and glucose to help them work normally.

187

Gestational Diabetes   The type of diabetes that occurs during pregnancy. Sometimes this diabetes goes away after delivery but sometimes it does not.

Glucagon   A hormone produced in the pancreas (by cells that are different from those that produce insulin). Glucagon is also packaged as a prescription drug that is given by injection to raise blood sugar levels during a serious insulin reaction. (The pancreas produces several hormones.)

Glucose   A sugar. It is a fuel for the cell, which changes glucose into energy. Most food that we eat is changed into glucose.

Glycohemoglobin Test   A test done by the doctor that can show how well your blood sugar has been controlled over the past month or two. It is the same as a hemoglobin A_{1C}, or glycosylated hemoglobin, test.

Hemoglobin A_{1C} Test   See *Glycohemoglobin Test.*

Hormone   A substance produced by a gland (and released into the bloodstream) that helps the body to work normally. Insulin is a hormone.

Hypoglycemia   See *Insulin Reaction.*

Immune Reaction   A response of the immune system to something that threatens the body. The immune system attempts to protect the body from infection.

Insulin   A hormone produced by the pancreas. Insulin helps sugar get into cells, where it can be changed into energy. Everyone needs to have insulin to stay alive. If people do not make enough in their own bodies, then they must replace it by taking insulin injections.

Insulin Reaction   When the sugar level in the blood falls too low—usually because of too much insulin, not enough food, or a lot of exercise. During an insulin reaction, most people feel hungry, sweaty, nervous, or weak.

Ketoacidosis   Also called diabetic coma. It occurs when the blood sugar gets very high and there is not enough insulin for the body. This sometimes happens before diabetes is diagnosed. Later it can happen for many reasons, including illness (such as the flu). It is a serious problem and needs quick attention by a doctor. High levels of ketones are a sign of impending ketoacidosis. (*Keto* comes from ketones; *acidosis* means the buildup of acids.)

Ketones   The waste product produced in the body when there is not enough insulin. (See *Acetone.*)

Ophthalmologist   A licensed physician who is also an eye doctor. Ophthalmologists have M.D. degrees. Optometrists don't; they check vision and fit people for glasses. People who have had diabetes for years need checkups by an ophthalmologist.

Organ   A part of the body. The liver, heart, brain, and pancreas are all organs.

Pancreas   The gland (organ) in the body that produces insulin. It lies behind the stomach in the abdomen.

Type I Diabetes   Insulin-dependent diabetes, in the past called juvenile-onset diabetes. The type of diabetes that always requires daily insulin shots.

Type II Diabetes   Non-insulin-dependent diabetes, in the past called maturity-onset diabetes. It is usually related to obesity and is generally treated effectively by weight loss alone. Sometimes it is also treated with pills (to help the pancreas to make more insulin and to help cells use insulin more effectively) or with insulin injections.

Urine   The yellow liquid (pee) that comes out of the bladder when you go to the bathroom.

Viral Infection   Sickness caused by a virus. Viruses cause many different kinds of infections, most commonly colds, sore throats, and the flu. Some viruses may help to cause diabetes.

The Diabetic Chocolate Cookbook, by Mary Jane Finsand, mentioned on page 99, is published by Sterling Publishing Company, Inc. of New York.

How To Have Your Cake And Eat It, Too! by Norma M. MacRae, R. D., mentioned on page 119, is published by Alaska Northwest Publishing Company.